Funny Old World

Lucy Ware

Published by New Generation Publishing in 2017

Copyright © Lucy Ware 2017

First Edition

The author asserts the moral right under the Copyright, Designs and Patents Act 1988 to be identified as the author of this work.

All Rights reserved. No part of this publication may be reproduced, stored in a retrieval system or transmitted, in any form or by any means without the prior consent of the author, nor be otherwise circulated in any form of binding or cover other than that which it is published and without a similar condition being imposed on the subsequent purchaser.

www.newgeneration-publishing.com

New Generation Publishing

List of Contents

Introduction 1

Chapter 1 - In the Beginning 3

Chapter 2 - Here We Go 9

Chapter 3 - New Friends...................................... 18

Chapter 4 - Consultation...................................... 28

Chapter 5 - Beside the Sea................................... 33

Chapter 6 - Dialogue with Doris.......................... 36

Chapter 7 - The Strange Case of Dr Zani 43

Chapter 8 - You Can't Choose Your Family 48

Chapter 9 - A Fourth Treatment 58

Chapter 10 - Local Business................................ 62

Chapter 11 - Medics – Another Breed................ 68

Chapter 12 - Lunch at Ciao Bellini..................... 73

Chapter 13 - Stateside.. 76

Chapter 14 - A Second Retreat 80

Chapter 15 - A Date with Dracula? 85

Chapter 16 - Goodbye Boots and All That 90

Chapter 17 - Mother at the Hospital 94

Chapter 18 - Travel Notes 98

Chapter 19 - Oh Buddha and HMS Disaster! ... 104

Chapter 20 - Fin du livre 110

*For two very important people – Frederick Walters and
Amanda Green*

Introduction

If you're like me, you probably won't read this introduction until you've finished the book. However, you'll probably take a quick look at the dedication because it's usually shorter. If this is the case, I would like to point out the reference made to Amanda Green for she was the inspiration for starting 'the book'. We had steered each other through difficult times via letter and telephone calls over the years and worked together for four of them before she moved back 'up north'. I'd witnessed her change from a young graduate fresh out of training, to an assertive, sophisticated force to be reckoned with.

Although we actually worked pretty hard most days, our office had never been short of laughter whilst Amanda was there. I taught her to become a workaholic and from her I learnt to value myself, put work in perspective and to look for humour in every difficult situation. Whenever I found myself taking life too seriously I'd hear her husky northern tones in my head telling me, *it's only WEARK!*

This book stemmed from a letter I'd sent her when I was depressed after being housebound through the winter months with a neck and shoulder injury. Hitting 'a high', I wrote to Amanda and despite putting my shoulder out of action for the rest of the week, found I couldn't stop wanting to write. Amanda suggested I write a book, but being unable to do too much physically at the time, I recorded some text and had it typed up later. That first letter was therapy for me at that time, as I sat in a quiet, religious retreat centre and laughed so much to myself I feared the wrath of the Lord.

I hope that parts of this book make my friend laugh now, as much as I did back then. If you find something in it too, then 'my cup overfloweth'.

3 April 2017

Chapter 1

In the Beginning

Dear Amanda,

I'm glad everything has been is going well since the house move and you are happy living closer to your relatives. I never told you this at the time, but I think it was very selfish of you moving away so quickly. Change can be a very traumatic thing for some people of my age and although I do my best to stay being a lively 'Une femme entre deux ages', sometimes life gets me down, and I miss you being around to cheer me up. I know Derm misses London, he told me so himself, so if you weren't thinking of your own husband when you moved away, who were you thinking of?

You always keep so much to yourself, but I can't and have to tell you I am not happy about a few things. For one thing, we didn't have enough beer and shopping trips together and I miss you telling me to take a lunch break (though I suppose I should let that one go as I am off sick), but look what happened since you left. That venetian blind fell on my head in the office and now I'm practically a disabled pensioner (well, maybe I do have a few years to go for that one). Nevertheless, if you'd been there it wouldn't have happened as that used to be your seat by the window not mine, and you're younger than me. The blind would probably have landed on that leather rucksack you kept on the back of your chair.

I might never forgive you.
Love,
B (PS not in a good mood!)

Bea,

Here's your last letter as promised. Thought I'd return the whole thing – you never know it might become a really important historical document one day.

Hope you're having a good day, talk to you soon.

Love,
Amanda
Ps I'm off shopping today with my credit card at the ready!

The Eden Centre
East Delling,
Kent

Hi Amanda,
Greetings from East Delling.!

I thought I'd put myself in an old people's home to save my kids the trouble, but I'm trying it out first. It's certainly better than the past three months at Hereford Road. The room's decorated; I can see horses from my window instead of traffic, but there's no commode ha ha.

Don't be shocked, I'm not really in an old folk's home but at a convent retreat centre for a break and to 'find the inner me'. Eric dropped me off at 10.30am; couldn't wait to get rid of me so he could dash down to the boat. (Of course he couldn't finish decorating the dining room, he only started that on December 15 last year and it's only March now.)

There's no telephone for incoming calls in the building and I've left my mobile at home. I haven't seen a television around, not that I could watch it for long, but I've got my German language CDs for company and if they answer me back at least I won't be able to understand what they say. It's 11.50am now, and lunch is at 12.30pm. I mustn't be long writing this letter or I might get a penance of doing the washing up and I couldn't take that.

I have been feeling odder than usual since my arrival. During my first fifteen minutes at this place I collected a bouquet of flowers from someone at the door; I couldn't find anyone to give them to nor remember which room I was in. Finally though, I did find someone to relieve me of the flowers and take me to my room (No.47), which I have written down to carry around with me in future, although I'm going home tomorrow night (if Eric ever remembers to pick me up again).

Love from here,
B

The Eden Centre
East Delling,
Kent

Hi Amanda,

I bet you were surprised to learn where I had gone for my 'therapeutic break' and expect you wonder what I'm really doing here – perhaps not. Maybe our pal Mark was right when he called me Sister Bea of the ovaries. (He had vision, that boy.) Well, I was (guess what) stressed out. Finally, I had some treatment (cost me a day's pay), with a Homeopathic Physician. He, and all the staff, looked like Buddhists to me. They didn't have bald heads, but an unhealthy look of serenity. Anyway, the day after treatment I felt relaxed, but achy in strange places and sort of Diazapam-ish without the tablets. The chief 'Buddhist' had given me some acupuncture which sent me on a strange high for a couple of days and then a 'downer'.

Aches and pains everywhere for a while then I felt better than before, very strange.

When you go to a homeopath they ask loads of questions and because it is all meant to be so healthy and natural, sometimes I was afraid to open my mouth (only for a while though). At my consultation I shamefacedly owned up that I sometimes drank two glasses of wine a week, had taken painkillers and two and a half mgs of Diazepam at night to relax my neck muscles. Also, I smoked about TEN CIGARETTES A DAY! Absolutely no comment was made but I felt I had lived a life of debauchery, so when all the pains came on again later, I didn't want to take anything for them. I felt back to square one, and really in the doldrums. That's when I decided I had to get away, rest my shoulders and SORT MY HEAD OUT FOR ONCE.

In my desperation for somewhere cheap and peaceful to go for a day or so, I discovered this place. I rang the night before and spoke to a lovely Jamaican girl, a teacher who helps out here in the evenings. She was so amusing and sympathetic, yet practical. She informed me that she was a civilian, not a nun, and that the rooms were not like cells and that I should take a look and stay if I wanted. My bag was packed before Eric could wake up from his after-work nap and when he finally surfaced I announced that I was going on my holidays to East Delling. I also rang my daughter-in-law, Dee, to explain that I wouldn't be around just in case she and Ned were to send me a Mother's day card with me not there to receive it, nor to phone them up and thank them. You have to be careful of such omissions when you're a mother in law!

I think Dee now believes that I've been adopted by some dodgy sect as she sounded rather quiet and bemused when I explained my plans for the weekend.

Well, here I am and my sense of humour has come back already. While I was winning I thought I'd make you laugh too instead of the usual whining. Anyway, I have an idea something will happen after this weekend; I don't know what, but I feel a premonition coming on (I hope it's not another slipped disc).

One-thirty and just finished my lunch. They sat me on the STAFF table. Imagine promotion already without so much as a CV. I don't think they'll keep me on though.

The man next to me introduced himself to me as Anthony Cribbing (I had to keep telling myself it wasn't Hopkins). I asked him if he were there for the weekend as I thought he might be a fellow inmate, but he told me he was the chaplain and probably thought I was chatting him up.

Got lost again on the way to my room, but was helped to find it by a kindly gentleman who had just walked in, and found me in a quandary.

Well I'm off now to talk to the horses and anyone else I come across. I keep laughing to myself and this place is meant to be quiet! It's a good job I'm going home tomorrow, as I'd probably be asked to leave anyway. Do you think I've been listening to too many old Tony Hancock tapes? Well, 'stone me', I hope not, but I do feel a bit odd. Perhaps on my next visit I'll try the sheltered accommodation down the road (St, Anne's). My friend, Anthony Hopkins (Cribbins) said it's quite good and takes people from all denominations. I wonder how they take to Buddhism?

Speak to you soon,
Love,
B

PS

By the way, I hope you appreciate this letter Amanda, because the envelope was very expensive. One of the nuns had told me to take anything I wanted and 'just put some money in the box'. I was amazed at this simple trust and honesty. Thinking the envelopes were worth about forty-five pence I felt generous putting in seventy-five. Later on I found the mark-up price was ONE POUND FORTY-FIVE PENCE! As I only had a ten pound note there were a few complications to deal with as I tried to figure out how to get change when the tin was empty. Should I buy a few more expensive envelopes or religious trinkets and paraphernalia or leave a donation? Eventually, pure philanthropy got the better of me; I left the tenner in the tin and hoped the next punter would be an honest one.

'Bye again.
B

Hiya B,

Thanks for the emergency life saver letters. As you can see by the card we're both away getting a bit of R and R and TLC and it's been great. Although the Retreat Centre sounds cool I'm not sure it is what I need at present. Not quite sure what I need – normality I think! Anyway, the last few days in Northumbria have been excellent. We're off to Beamish and then home today. It's not sunny today but Derm's still got his shorts on!

Take care,
Love to Eric,
Amanda and Dermot xx

Chapter 2

Here We Go

The Eden Centre
East Delling,
Kent

Dear Amanda,

As usual, I've decided to do as you told me in your letter and write everything down (for therapeutic purposes) and thought you might like to see what's been done with it so here goes...

I have deposited myself in a convent to recuperate from the terrible wounds inflicted by a Venetian blind. Additionally, I am here for a while to escape from life's stresses and the weariness of the world and to find the true meaning of my existence. The surroundings are pleasant if sparse, the food adequate if wanting in a certain piquancy, the company most ahem... interesting. I'm sure I shall gain much from this experience and leave here a better person (or, here will be better after this person has left). Indeed, this is truly a marvellous place for cleansing the soul, opening one's heart and finding contentment.

Unfortunately, it's Mother's Day tomorrow and I bet everybody else gets flowers! One of my boys doesn't know I'm here and my husband is out on the seven seas (OK river) so I'll be miserable. Well, at least I can go and have a cigarette in the grounds or, as the note on the wall says, 'by the telephone area in inclement weather'.

Saturday

It was wishful thinking about that quick smoke yesterday for after leaving me here my dearly beloved had sped off in the car with the Guardian newspaper and cigarettes he'd so thoughtfully bought me. Not that he was in a hurry to leave me of course, but the call of the river was just too much for him. All at once I felt dejected, unloved and dumped taking second place to a boat in his affections. I quickly got a grip on my feelings and told myself that if I wanted a cigarette I'd better go out and look for some. After all I wasn't exactly marooned even though it felt like it. Putting on my surgical collar and my jacket I set out to look for newsagents. After leaving the grounds of the retreat centre I found myself in suburbia and asked a boy on a skateboard where to find the nearest shop. He issued me with what seemed rather complicated directions for my vulnerable brain but I latched on to the bit about the pathway through the park.

After a few minutes' walk I found the park and a narrow path which crossed two rugby pitches with games in play on either side of it. Just my luck! I quickly weighed up the probability of both balls hitting me in the neck at the same time. Driven on by the nicotine withdrawal symptoms I judged this disaster to be unlikely and continued on my way, staring straight ahead and keeping my fingers crossed. Once through the park everything seemed brighter. A man pushing a baby along in a pram smiled at me, flowers were in bloom in all the gardens, the sun was shining and suddenly spring had arrived. I wondered about that man's smile, did he have a penchant for pasty faced fat women or was it a sympathetic smile for the surgical collar? Funny too about the weather. Just six miles away and a few hours earlier in Hereford Road it had still been winter. Maybe the climate was milder in East Delling.

A few minutes later I'd found a newsagents, bought a paper, my precious cigarettes and a packet of chewing gum to disguise my distasteful habit from the nuns. I had a smoke, then a gum. YUK! Liquorice flavour. Was this my penance for finding the cigarette shop? I wondered whether to have another cigarette before my precarious return through the two rugby pitches but decided against it. I'd save it as a treat for later. Surely I'd be able to locate 'the smoking area by the telephone booth' on my return to the centre. If I'd known then what I was about to encounter during the course of the evening I'd have smoked the whole pack.

Returning to the centre after my venture into town, I reached the peace and tranquillity of my room where I lay down on the bed and made an ambitious attempt at reading the newspaper for a few minutes before dropping off to sleep. It was difficult to read at the table for fear of getting my neck stuck and I didn't manage to do it in bed either as I was asleep before reaching the end of the first line. It must have been quite a slumber as it was almost supper time when I awoke and strangely my Guardian newspaper seemed to have disappeared. I didn't have time to pay much attention to this detail as I quickly got ready to join my new companions for supper.

Helping myself to food at the hatch I sat down at the staff table where all 'individuals' sat. The room thronged with voices as a group party arrived to eat. At lunch I had overheard Sister Teresa tell someone very quietly that she thought that today's group might be a bit 'OTT'. (Code letters for over the top.) I had no idea then what she meant but was soon to discover her meaning exactly. During the meal I chatted away to various people and was introduced to Ellen, a nun from Dublin with whom I immediately hit it off. I noticed a woman with blue steely eyes approach Sr. Teresa. They exchanged a few words and it was obvious that they already knew each other. After supper

Ellen asked me if I intended to go along to the evening meeting. I said I was interested but didn't know what it was about. When she told me it was about faith healing I thought I'd make an attempt at sitting it out and leave early if the pains came on (o yea of little faith).

Entering the meeting I found myself sitting next to 'Steel Eyes'. Sr. Teresa beckoned me over to the other side of the room to sit beside her. I was really getting into my role of being 'on the staff', but knew she was really just trying to make me feel at ease.

Eight o'clock in the evening, and the kindly gentleman who had shown me to my room earlier on appeared to be the leader of the group meeting. We sat around in a big circle and were treated to an enactment of 'The Easter Message' by two children. When it was over the children were applauded and 'Leader' began to preach. He talked of the terrible things happening in the world to our children and how in spite of this evil we should find forgiveness. At this point I shot 'Leader' a glance in case he was a child molester and I know he had caught me looking at him, but 'Leader' went on to talk about the troubles in Northern Ireland. He thought that there was a lot of goodness in that place so, plenty of work for the Devil to do (apparently). When the Devil was quiet as in England he said there was little to keep him occupied because work was already complete. I could see 'Leader's' point on this as I'd had some first-hand experience of some pretty evil people. There was always someone out to get you in this world. No one was safe, not even old ladies with sticks like my mother, although I have to admit there were quite a few people who were afraid of her, (me for one). All in all, I could go along with a lot of 'Leader's' views but wasn't too sure about agreeing with his next statement. L said we should be aware of all the non-Christian religions springing up in the UK. While these worshippers were to be respected he said, it should be a warning to us of the Devil's work already under way! *Hang on*, I thought, hadn't a similar type of religious bigotry contributed to the 'troubles' in Northern Ireland? The group intended to go there to try and unite two Christian religions. Was it OK then to unite against non-Christian faiths? Especially since Christians couldn't keep their own houses in order? I decided to keep quiet at all costs and just watch the proceedings.

A few moments later, the healing part of the meeting commenced and we were all asked to turn to the right and put our hand on the shoulder of the person sitting next to us. Sr. Teresa sat on my right and a blue shirted young man on my left. We were then requested to pray for 'healing' for the person we were touching. I thought Sr. Teresa looked very healthy and happy to me but prayed to heal whatever might be wrong with her just in case. Soon, I felt a hot heavy hand on my good shoulder (the left one) as 'Blue Shirt' concentrated hard and prayed to have me healed. A strange chant left his lips and I could only discern it as sounding something like 'Kyria Korie, Kyria Korie, Kyria, Kyria, Korie'. I found myself mesmerised by his words and tried to make out which language he was speaking. It didn't sound like Latin but that was the closest I could put it at (unless it was Esperanto) and realised with guilt, that I was more taken up with having a stab at a translation than sorting out Sr. Teresa's ailments. Before I was taken too far into this guilt trip, we were quickly asked to turn to our left and return the compliment. I placed my hand on 'Blue Shirt' and felt myself reassured by the light, sensible touch of Sr. Teresa on my 'bad shoulder'. She was asking the Lord to sort me out if he saw fit. Trying to translate Kyria Korie and think about Whether Sr. Teresa's prayer was working I panicked in the realisation that I was selling 'Blue Shirt' short as I had placed my hand on the wrong shoulder. The one that had already been done by the person on his other side! I quickly swapped my hand to his other shoulder and hoped that BS would forgive me and that I hadn't spoilt the healing circle. After this activity, candles were lit and placed on a small table in the middle of our circle. A few people dropped to their knees around the candles whilst some others went across and put their hands on the heads of the kneelers.

Steel Eyes came across and indicated to Sr. Teresa that one young man kneeling down was feeling particularly unhappy. His parents had 'shut down' all communication with him. Sr. Teresa went over and reluctantly, I thought, placed her kindly hands on his head. It was difficult for me to contain myself at this point. I felt a compulsion to rush over, pull the lad to his feet, get to the bottom of it all and suggest ways that he could get back into his parents' favour. It seems I really did miss interviewing all those unemployed miserable kids at work. Wisely, I decided to stick to my plan of watching all during the meeting and saying nothing. There was plenty to watch alright, a lot of wailing, exchanging of stories and repentance. It wasn't long before my neck began to ache through sitting upright for so long and I felt tired and drained. Communicating with the Lord was heady stuff. Suddenly, a woman leapt to her feet and said she had to repent for Kenya, on account of having been nursed there as a child by some 'kindly black people' and there had been some dreadful atrocities in Kenya.

I found this all very confusing as well as disturbing. I'd only come for a quiet weekend to get over the acupuncture and could have done with having a few needles on me myself, to shut them all up! Dr Ling could have made a fortune (if he didn't have one already of course). I began to toy with the idea of offering him my services as a paid Business Consultant when I became fit. Everybody was becoming a consultant these days; it was the one job you didn't seem to need any particular qualifications for. From what I could gather, the main attributes necessary were to have plenty of chat and to be on the scrap heap. The job spec seemed to fit me quite well. I could go round to all the retreat centres seeking out hysterical religious zealots as patients for Dr L. There were a lot of retreat centres in Europe too, especially in Rome and Paris, my two favourite cities. I'd quite like visiting all those places picking up 'sick' people and marketing his acupuncture treatments. Of course, Dr L's ethics would probably only allow him to see those who also had muscular-skeletal problems. Hmm... maybe I could charge a bit extra for categorising them and offer those who were muscularly and skeletally fit to Judy, the acupuncturist at the Wise Care Health Centre? A double whammy for me! I decided to reserve these business ideas until my neck was cured and would give it more thought later. Meanwhile, I would continue to listen and look on at what was going on around me. I was doing precisely that and nursing my shoulder when, suddenly, my nerves were shattered by another woman to my right who burst into a fit of uncontrollable tears. Speaking with a foreign accent, she announced that she had to repent for her country: Switzerland. Puzzled by this, I saw 'Blue Shirt' go across to her and say he understood. His Polish-Jewish grandmother had lost all her wealth in that country during the war, he said. I'd recalled something about this in the news recently (not about 'Blue Shirt's' grandmother, but about people losing money in Switzerland during the war). Unaware of the background details, I didn't find this sufficient reason for the distress that this woman was displaying and must have looked worried and puzzled as I certainly felt that way. While 'Blue Shirt' comforted the Swiss woman, 'Leader' walked across to me and said that he couldn't explain why, but something told him he needed to inform me that I possessed great insight and that I 'knew truth'. I could explain why to him alright. L probably noticed me eyeballing him earlier when, I'd suspected him of being a child molester! 'Leader' said the Lord had something he wanted me to do. Feeling myself on some other plane and speaking with a voice that wasn't my own, I asked L if he could please find out for me what it was. Placing his hand on my head, L prayed out loud and for me to discover what it was I 'was called to do' and I thought I could feel some kind of 'presence' close to me (apart from myself and 'Leader' that is).

Happy and confident in the knowledge that I had a new found 'gift' I decided to go over and console 'Switzerland'. I seemed to be in a sort of religious haze and felt like a cross between Billy Graham and Yuri Geller. I'd always wanted to be able to bend spoons like he did, just by stroking them. The only way I'd managed to do this in the past was by accidentally getting them jammed in the cutlery drawer at home.

Taking hold of 'Switzerland's' hand, I asked her if she would please explain to me the business about her country. Had her grandmother had the same problem with the Swiss as 'Blue Shirt'? 'No,' she answered, but she was upset about the Nazis that had operated from there etc. Feeling myself at home now and getting into counselling mode, I advised her that she couldn't possibly take on all the guilt for the whole of Switzerland. That such things were now history and not 'her own stuff' anyway, but someone else's'. It was no good, she was hell bent on repentance and refused to be helped – she was definitely stuck in denial. I could see that. Desperate to console, I asked her name, which she said was Celine. I told her about the book I had read at school once. There had been a character with her name in it who'd helped African slaves escape from North America to Canada. Celine smiled at this and seemed to cheer up a bit, much to my relief. I had been determined to use my new gift as soon as I could before it disappeared (like my copy of the Guardian from my room)!

Shortly after our little talk, the meeting finished and I walked out from the building with Switzerland and across the small square outside. We bade each other goodnight and S turned off to the right, I to the left, but found myself walking once more, in the wrong direction. 'Plus ça change' there! Eventually, I located the door to my building (where Switzerland had gone in the first place). On entry I was greeted by Ellen, who asked me to help her lock up as she wanted to help Sr. Teresa but couldn't quite manage the doors due to the arthritis in her hands. After several attempts at using my right arm that was giving me gyp, I concluded that I couldn't manage the doors either. In the end we both gave up and left the job to Sr. Teresa, who had just come down the corridor. I said goodnight to the two of them after admitting that I'd got lost again on the way over. Sr. Teresa smiled and said that I was completely hopeless wasn't I? 'Yes,' I affirmed to this insult. I had to agree she was right, but I was also knackered, and took myself off to bed.

Chapter 3

New Friends

Sunday, the following day, had a most confusing start to it. Arriving for breakfast at 8am, I found that the furniture had been moved around and there was no staff table for me to sit at. There weren't many people about either, my Catholic brethren had all gone to the inter-denominational service to help Christian unity. This meant that they had two services to attend, the 'C of E' type one as well as their own RC 9am Mass.

I helped myself to cornflakes and sat down at another table only to discover that I had taken the place reserved for a young man in a wheelchair. His helper gave me an understanding smile and whisked his charge away to breakfast elsewhere. A few minutes later I was joined by a sensible looking smiling, middle-aged woman. I apologised to her nervously, excusing myself for being at the table because I had found no 'staff table' for people who were 'individuals' to sit at, and owned up that I was 'an individual'. She smiled at this saying that she too was an 'individual', only one visiting with a group! I smiled too, and explained that I normally occupied a unique position on the staff table but that it had disappeared (along with that copy of the Guardian from my room that I kept thinking about). My table companion turned out to be Joan, a teacher from Lancashire, who was a very committed Charismatic Catholic. Her interesting conversation about the Charismatic movement was very convincing and I liked her. J asked if I knew how she could find a retreat centre nearer to her home. My geography and memory of the AA map seemed vague but with false confidence I suggested the Holy Isle. 'No,' she said, that was too far north. Ever helpful, I suggested she ask one of the nuns or look in the Universe Catholic Newspaper. Later, Eric asked me why the hell someone from Lancashire should choose to ask someone from South East London directions for her own county, but I had no answer to that question. I just accepted the fact that people always asked me questions, whether I could answer them or not.

In my time I'd been approached by countless people seeking information or advice; foreign tourists, bag ladies even a lost millionaire on a train (or so he said) and I never thought to ask why he hadn't come by private helicopter. Once, a passenger on a cross channel ferry tried to order a gin and tonic off me because I was wearing a blue dress with brass buttons and looked like a crew member. At my son's graduation I was taken for a ceremony official and kept being asked questions and directions because someone spotted me wandering about with a programme under my arm and had a round, silver, brooch on my jacket which people thought was a badge. Another time, on holiday in Majorca, a German tourist come up to me and asked if she could change her hotel room because the noise from the disco kept her awake. As I hadn't been able to understand what she was saying her daughter was summoned to attempt an English translation. I managed to make out that this woman and her grown up family were on a package deal holiday and accompanied by dozens of their compatriots. The situation became a bit complicated because I only spoke a smattering of German so tried to persuade them to converse in French which I might deal with better. I was just preparing myself to try out my few words of Spanish on the hotel manager for my German friends, when Eric arrived and became involved in the situation too. He sorted out the whole confusion within minutes by using sign language and speaking in English. E became a temporary hero and whenever we saw the woman again she would wink at him, raise her glass at the dinner table, or say 'Guten Tag' at breakfast.

Regardless of what happened in Majorca though, Eric had raised a good a point about the teacher from Lancashire. It crossed my mind whether she had received a tip off from 'Leader' about my 'knowing truth' and thought this gift could be applied to directions 'up north' as well!

Joan had given me an invitation to what sounded like another mind bending spiritual experience. Fortunately, I was able to inform her that I would be leaving at 6pm and therefore, couldn't avail myself of it and anyway, I told her, that I thought I'd keep to the more conservative stuff.

After breakfast, I tried to make my way to Mass but not being able to find the chapel was soon taken charge of by a plump dark-haired woman wearing an Alice band. Unfortunately, it shortly became apparent that we were both lost when Alice Band said she knew where the chapel was, if only she could remember! *Hello*, I thought, *someone with my problem*. Eventually we arrived at Mass where I seated myself at the back of the church so that I could leave early if my neck pain started. Alice Band had first chosen a seat for herself down at the front and then left it again to come and apologise for not being able to sit beside me. I explained that it was alright because I wanted a quick means of escape on account of my sore neck. AB confided that she needed an equally fast means of escape to the toilet and that the front pew was the best position for this. We commiserated and exchanged knowing sympathetic smiles before Alice Band returned to her seat.

Surprisingly, we both made it through the short service but on my exit from chapel Alice Band hurried up to me apologising again for not having sat next to me during the mass. This omission was apparently due to her irritable bowel syndrome. By the time we reached the main building I had discovered not only that she occupied the room next to me but half her life history as well. AB did indeed have a sad tale to tell and I was treated to every detail of it in full.

My new acquaintance had been a child in what was then, war-torn Belfast. Her teenage years apparently, traumatised by family servitude and slavery, skeletons in cupboards and sectarian violence, which had destroyed her mental state and seemed to be about to do the same to mine. Two hours later, I was not only still listening but also holding her hand and doing a bit more counselling again while she tearfully let the whole mess of it all out to me. I girded my loins and listened to all AB's health problems too. I felt I couldn't let her down and as usual, was confident of being able to help in some way. Unfortunately, the spirit as they say was 'willing' but the flesh wasn't up to it as I felt the whole of my neck, head and shoulders begin to disintegrate. Sitting up straight in the chapel hadn't done much for them and I now needed to lie down – no chance! I felt compelled to hang on for as long as possible while Alice Band went on to tell me about her HRT problem, the arthritis in her feet, forthcoming hysterectomy and the after effects of coming off antidepressants, AND DIAZAPAM!

Throughout this 'consultation' we had been standing in Alice Band's bedroom which I noticed was littered with piles of literature about various obscure Christian movements. AB said that the charismatic programme over the weekend had all been too much for her. Just part of it had been too much for me and I only had a neck problem. Apart from the aforementioned ailments there were two other big worries in A's life. She desperately wanted to sing in Belfast on the eve of St. Patrick as a prayer for world peace only feared she wouldn't be well enough for it. A also had planned an overnight stay with friends in Canary Wharf. On the other hand she was so heartbroken about the IRA explosion which had taken place there a few years earlier and seemed to be going along on the same guilt trip as Switzerland had the evening before! Alice Band was trying to take responsibility for the residents of Canary Wharf not having received any compensation for the damage. AB seemed so physically and mentally ill that I almost felt like calling a doctor, only I wasn't sure which one of us he'd need to treat first. After Alice Band had expelled all her immediate problems, I suggested we go to the kitchen for a cup of coffee. I guessed they'd be out of alcohol as the all Irish group expected hadn't yet arrived. (You got to know about such things sitting on the staff table.)

In the kitchen we were met by Steel Eyes, who comforted Alice Band too and told her that she didn't appear fit enough to visit any friends in Canary Wharf. I was quite relieved to think she might take over my role here for I badly needed the break. Steel Eyes informed me she visited the retreat centre fairly often as she only lived down the road. Her poor husband hadn't been converted yet, she said, but she was obviously working on him. Steel Eyes asked me where I lived and with a wheedling look, asked for my telephone number. Caught unawares, I somehow didn't feel able to refuse it but self-preservation thoughts quickly took over and I gave her Eric's old business number. The one we'd had three years ago when we still had a business and some money. If the Lord had given me the strength to counsel Alice Band, it seemed the Devil was helping me out now with Steel Eyes. Excusing myself from them both, I said I had to go and pack and dashed out of the kitchen while Steel Eyes was 'being mother' with the tea and the instant coffee.

Once inside my bedroom, I locked the door and collapsed on the bed to recover myself and do some thought gathering. Yes, I would have to escape as soon as possible, my time of realisation and self-discovery had come to an end. If I reached home quick enough it might still be possible to hang on to some of the therapeutic effects of the 'rest' before they were extinguished completely. After all, I didn't want to waste the twenty-seven pounds I was soon due to pay out for the privilege of being there.

My next move was to get up and locate a telephone. I soon found this plus the smoking area for times of 'inclement weather'. I tried to ring my knight in shining armour on his mobile phone, without success. Eric was obviously still down at the boat, with his means of emergency communications switched off as usual, to save the batteries. What kind of logic did that man use I asked myself? Yes, I knew he didn't really care what happened to me in this place and he'd driven off with my Guardian and cigarettes and I hated him forever. The thought of the cigarettes offered a sudden solution. I'd walk through the park, have a smoke and phone him again later.

I took off once more for the park and this time I was in luck. There was just a trickle of rain and no rugby in play. Brilliant! By the time I had reached the path, however, I was about to undergo yet another test. No rugby balls this time but a big, black, dangerous looking Doberman. Large dogs came about third place on my list of phobias almost on a par with swimming and flying. This dog looked the worst sort possible. I could tell by the way he let his head hang loose that he was a free spirit, an unpredictable kind of hound. The type usually held on the end of a piece of string by a punk rocker or one of those ex-sixties flower power people you see at music festivals. I realised this judgement hadn't been too far out when I spotted the owner; a leather jacketed, chain dangling teenager, loitering around with a few other unsavoury looking characters. If only he'd had the dog attached to the chain things wouldn't have been so bad. As it was, I decided to detour the path and keep myself out of the dog's view by walking behind a small brick building that looked like a changing room.

Dogs could smell cowards a mile away but I hoped the rain would help to confuse its senses a bit. Walking behind the building, I noticed a teenage girl and boy huddled together against a brick wall. Averting my eyes I stared straight ahead and pretended I'd seen nothing. I guessed that they were either taking drugs or having sex. Having no experience of one and only a faded recollection of the other, I wasn't sure, so I kept going and prayed that I would neither be beaten up for drug money nor met at the corner of the brick wall by the black Doberman.

Reaching the exit gates to the park and having escaped both hazards I breathed a sigh of relief, lit a cigarette and pondered on being in suburbia again but SMOKING IN A STREET! I was glad of being unknown in the area; a bit of a snob when it came to walking in the street with a lit cigarette. After a few puffs I extinguished the cigarette and continued along to the town centre found a telephone booth and attempted to make another call to my boat crazy husband, without success. No luck, he was still saving on the batteries. Lighting up another cigarette to regain renewed courage and face the dog and teenage rebels in the park, I turned to go back the way I'd come. Eureka! The coast seemed to be clear from all animal and human threat and within a few minutes I'd arrived back at the retreat centre again.

Later that day I did eventually manage to get through to my uncaring husband via the telephone by the smoking area reserved for 'inclement weather'. E's calm response that he would be with me in twenty minutes was the best thing I'd heard all day. I forgave him everything as we drove the six miles home and he listened to me gabble on about all that had happened. Chattering away I was impressed how calmly he'd taken it all without interrupting me once. I looked at Eric and noticed the glazed over expression on his face. He was on automatic pilot again, with all means of communication shut down to save the batteries! I stopped talking immediately and didn't utter another word. After all, who could blame him for it this time.

During the following week my mind felt wonderfully relaxed. I seemed to do and say things purely on instinct without giving any thought to the consequences. I began to anticipate things before they happened. I'd think of friends just before they rang me on the telephone or I'd make a call to them just as they were about to call me. One day I left a message on a friend's answerphone. She wasn't what you'd call a close friend and we hadn't been in touch for several months. She returned my call that same evening saying that she'd found my message quite eerie as she had thought about me several times during the day and wanted to call but never had the opportunity to do so. I had always been a bit like this and once had a premonition about the murder of Senator Robert Kennedy a year before it happened. I didn't really like this deep side of myself and didn't want to encourage it as it gave me the creeps.

One evening that week, I watched a TV programme about the search for a missing child. I was heavily engrossed in the programme when suddenly the details of a dream I'd had several years previously came into my mind. I felt that they related somehow to the case and immediately sat down to write to the people concerned and explain why I thought the dream details might be helpful to their search. I added that I was of sound mind and that if the information seemed like rubbish to them to just throw the letter away and think no more about it.

When Eric came in and saw what I was doing he was furious with me and said I was acting irresponsibly and giving people false hopes. I mentioned that I was also sending in a cheque for ten pounds to help with their travel expenses in case the information didn't prove helpful, but this didn't make him happy either. Anyway, after E turned me off the idea nothing was the same. I shoved the letter into a draw and tried to forget it. I told myself that acupuncture had made me feel relaxed and that the retreat centre and the incident with 'Leader' had just made me suggestible. When retelling all this later to my friend Julia she said everything seemed quite logical to her and that I should send the letter off. However, I couldn't quite bring myself to it so it's still in my desk drawer. I had told J that it was probably just a case of the acupuncture holes letting a few of my psychic tendencies escape and that they were best left where they were.

A few days later I received a telephone call from Dr Ling to find out how I had reacted to his treatment. Dr L was delighted to hear about the pains and the mood swings because it meant that encephalins had been released through the acupuncture treatment and said that pain could sometimes be a good thing (was he kidding or what?). Pain and mood swings apparently, were all very good signs that the acupuncture would eventually help my soft tissue damage. I let him know as tactfully as possible that with some pre-warning I might not have thought I had been going nuts! I found out later that it wasn't really Dr L's fault when I looked up some information for myself about acupuncture and found out that I am a 'strong reactor type'.

Apparently, fifteen per cent of patients are strong reactors and they are often sensitive, artistic, athletic or, highly intelligent people. When I told my office colleague Chris G. about this, she said, 'Why of course you are all of those things, aren't you.' *Huh!* I thought, another wind up at my expense. Even when I'm temporarily disabled people poke fun at me. I let her off though, because I like her and I was glad to have done so after discovering that another symptom of being an FR person is being a fast talker. Surely this couldn't be the only reason I had qualified? I felt as though I had just been awarded a low grade GCSE pass in a subject nobody had heard of. It couldn't be true could it? No. I was sensitive all right and also creative; I created all sorts of things, mainly complications for myself. I could loosely be termed artistic too. However, I probably wouldn't qualify under the intelligence heading and definitely not on the grounds of being athletic. Rather proud though at the speed I could run up a staircase and beat my friend Babs up the slope at the railway station whenever we were late for a train. I took great pleasure in beating her run on account of all the lectures she'd delivered me on giving up smoking.

That was one of the things I'd always liked about Amanda; she'd told me once that as I had been a smoker for so long my lungs were black anyway and I might as well carry on and enjoy it. For a non-smoking, non-caffeine drinking vegetarian, she is very liberal minded and always encourages people to do what they want. Her personal philosophy is: 'If it's not what you want, it's not gonna satisfy ya!' Which reminds me, it's about time I wrote some letters.

Dear Amanda,

You didn't reply to my message on the answer phone so I don't know whether you are on holiday or not. Your request to leave a message was very business-like so you can't be ill. In that case you'd have sounded husky and sad and be asking for people to say something cheerful to amuse you. I was caught out with that one before and sang you songs two weeks after you had recovered from flu and gone back to work without changing the message on the answerphone! No consideration sometimes.

Can you please let me know whether you are poorly, or away enjoying yourself?

Hope everything is OK,
Love, B

Chapter 4

Consultation

This time I had a better idea of what I was in for at the hospital so was fully prepared. With not much else to occupy me at home, I had come to prepare for these visits as though they were board meetings (though from the expression on his face Dr L might call them 'bored' meetings). I took along my X-ray and scans, a page of notes for Dr Ling (to keep him up to speed) and three pages of questions for me. I could have done with a briefcase really, if I had been able to hold it. I will definitely get a portfolio case for the X-rays. I have always fancied carrying one of those because it makes people wonder what is in them.

While waiting to go in the consulting room, I picked up some leaflets. One department was asking for volunteer bunion sufferers to take part in clinical trials for a treatment using Marigolds. As I only suffer from a corn I thought I might tell Sarah at work about it. Her walking holiday in Greece was ruined by a bunion. She and her husband Derek had a special ten-mile walk planned for themselves and Sarah had trained for it for weeks by walking three miles every evening. Unfortunately, by the time they arrived in Greece the bunion had had it, and gave out completely in the middle of the aforementioned planned trek. Derek had to carry her back to the hotel and they didn't speak to each other again for the rest of the holiday.

During our stint in the waiting room, Eric was busy reading things too. Only he never lets you know about it, and you would swear he were asleep or daydreaming if you looked at him. When we started to discuss the exercises I had been instructed to do for the last two weeks, he suddenly informed me that I had missed out the 'shoulder shrugs' he had seen Dr Ling demonstrate last time as he had watched from the adjoining room. At the time E had denied seeing anything. The shoulder shrug information must have disappeared somewhere into his subconscious, emerging just in time to get me into a panic a few minutes before I was due to go in for treatment.

Eric said he thought he might put his name down for the Chronic Fatigue Clinic which he'd just read a leaflet on. I think it's a good idea. I'd do anything to find a cure for it and get a few more words out of him. You might describe E as the strong, silent type. I might get Chris G to look up the symptoms for sleeping sickness in her Black's Medical Dictionary for me, just in case. I was pondering on Eric's Chronic Fatigue Syndrome when Dr Ling called my name out. I glanced up to see his billboard straight figure stationed a few feet away, his face totally expressionless. Encased in a stiff white coat he looked as though he had just been emulsioned. I felt that I ought to offer some type of salute or something but wasn't sure of the formality for Buddhists. While following Dr Ling into the consulting room, I apologised for not giving him enough information the last time. He hadn't explained what he was trying to establish and I hadn't realised he was taking the holistic approach. I had really got into it all now though and issued him with a foolscap page of notes detailing my lifestyle, health habits, etc. (not the smoking one). I had told him about that last time but hoped it had been forgotten. I did have to mention my mother, of course, but he didn't pick up on anything. I think natural remedists like old people; I had seen one in the waiting room. Anyway, Dr Ling seemed to appreciate the notes which were quite concise, having been whittled down from three foolscap sheets and said, 'Oh thank you, can I keep this?' as though he'd been given a Christmas present. I announced that I had some notes too in case he felt bad about it (one page of questions and three pages of background information). Dr L said that he would answer all my questions while he was doing the acupuncture and led me into the treatment room completely ignoring my protestations that I wouldn't be able to remember them without my list and the spectacles that I had left on his desk. I needn't have worried anyway, as my mind was suddenly forced to concentrate on the answers to his questions which were posed in rapid succession as he pinched and prodded my shoulder muscles, shoving in a needle here and there. My voice-box was like a record winding down as Dr L continued puncturing along various meridians with the needles. While he worked away I had a notion that he was trying to get his own back for having to put up with my chatter. He seemed to be in his element stabbing away at the same time delivering a running commentary on which muscles were where and what function they performed. I am sure he suspected that this was all a bit too technical for me to absorb with my weakened brain but the stabs did the trick and shut me up.

After the acupuncture was over and we had returned to his consulting room, I was like a zombie. I couldn't remember my new exercises and had to be shown again. I was mixed up with all the questions I had wanted to ask as Dr L seemed to answer two or three in one go so I kept losing the place on my checklist. The one important thing I should have reminded him of *before* the treatment was that I was a strong reactor. It was unfortunate to have left this out so I crossed my fingers and hoped things would be OK and that I wouldn't need to recuperate somewhere again, but who knew what might happen this time?

While Dr Ling sat at his desk making notes for next time, I told him that I hoped to go away with my sister for a few days if I were up to it. He seemed to be interested in my self-cure trips as he had asked me a lot of questions about the Retreat Centre. Anyway, I said that we might take a train to Bournemouth as I couldn't risk jogging my neck in a car or bus and watched him smile to himself. Maybe, he wondered why I wasn't doing another retreat. I hadn't mentioned the fact that Alice Band had done my head in. Dr L heartily approved of the new planned trip saying it would do me good to get the wind on my face and get in some walking. So I WAS pale after all, everyone had been lying to me about looking better.

As Dr Ling's weary face began to hold a more convivial expression, I was tempted to confide that we were mainly planning of sleeping without the pressure of friends and family around endeavouring to bring us back to normality. There was also a compulsion to tell him about my sister's anaemia and borderline thyroid problem, which would explain why she needed a rest too. I held control of myself as my 'people training' warned me that his might just be the last straw and too much information as they say. Perhaps enough to damage the fragile communication link that we had managed to establish. Holding back proved a difficult task and I suddenly had to put in: 'By the way, I've got a headache now.' The good doctor raised his head, glanced up at the spot I had indicated, nodded and looked down at his notes again.

Dr L gave me orders to take a hot shower when got home and warned me to be prepared for the same after effects as last time and added in a school masterly tone, 'I'm telling you so this time you'll know!' I almost advised him to go on the 'Improve your communication skills course' my work friend Ginny had delivered to some junior doctors just after her gynae op. Call me suspicious, but I have often wondered whether the doctors took up Ginny's offer so that they could psychoanalyse her. Ginny can talk for England and laughs a lot. In my experience, two things that doctors don't do much so might find rather strange.

They ought to spend some work experience time in our office for that!

Dr Ling carried on writing again. Wishing to be helpful, I offered up the notion that the injury to my little finger, which I had pulled by lifting up a briefcase a year ago, might throw some light on the shoulder problem. Hurting my little finger had caused a bit of swelling to the wrist but it was OK now, but just in case…. Laying down his biro with deliberation, Dr Ling took hold of my wrist, and turning his eyes away to face the blanked out glass windows, examined it very carefully; like a blind piano tuner fingering a keyboard. I'm not sure he appreciated my tip-off though, for after a few minutes he discarded the wrist, muttered that it was fine and gave me an appointment to see him again in three weeks' time. But why the long-time gap? I judged there could be one of three reasons for this:

1) The treatment was to have such a dramatic effect that I would need that amount of time to recover from it.

2) He was going on holiday.

3) He would need three weeks' break to recover from seeing me.

I'd hoped it was the second reason, but suspected it was the third and I left without asking any more questions. I expect Dr Ling went home and took a couple of Diazepam or gave himself a few stabs with the needles to take his mind off things as he now looked as though he needed treatment more than I did.

Perhaps it had been a long day for him. It felt like 5pm to me too but it turned out to be only 3.30pm – strange.

Chapter 5

Beside the Sea

So, we took off for Bournemouth, my poor long suffering anaemic sister with the borderline thyroid problem and me, with what Dr Ling called my 'Iffy' discs. Wearing my surgical collar to ward off any bumps or jogs caused by the train journey, I discovered a wonderful perk to wearing this appliance was that I had some very handsome young men offering to help me with my bag. It was amazing how much kindness there could be around and I was really looking forward to our long weekend.

The flat felt chilly when we first arrived but it was such a relief to be away from home and the memory of all those miserable winter months. It was still only March and quite windy but the view from our window was cheery and we were both AWAY! The following three days were spent taking long walks followed by long sleeps. It was great having no pressure to do anything other than what we felt up to doing. We took full advantage of our self-imposed convalescence by walking, resting and undertaking only the most necessary chores such as heating up the odd microwave meal or boil in the bag delights.

Back home once more and rejuvenated, I replied to Amanda's latest letter:

Dear Amanda,

I am only just replying because I have been away for a few days with my sister which did me a power of good.

Sorry to hear you have been feeling a bit 'down' in the dumps and sorry too, that I wasn't at the end of the phone for you as you have been so many times for me. I am sending you some tapes of some nutty music that helps me when feeling 'down': George Melly and Hoagy Carmichael – try it. As to thinking about the heartaches of last year, well it was a lousy year for many of my friends and maybe I know the reason. I forgot to plant the shamrock seeds that you sent me! So sorry about that but I might be able to help you out with your bunion. I have found out about a trial for a marigold cure at Dr Ling's clinic and am sending the information to Sarah so I will get you a leaflet on it too. Don't laugh at me, I am into all healthy natural stuff now (except giving up cigarettes and being teetotal). Isn't life strange? If I hadn't done my neck in I would never have been able to help you with your bunion. Anyway, if you can hop on to a train to London you can take part in the trials and be introduced to my Buddhist doctor. I don't see how you could have a bunion though as you always wear good shoes. I'd have a second opinion if I were you, Sarah spent years on stiletto heels so she has a reason for a bunion but you don't wear them.

I chatted to Eric's friend, Joe, about my idea of conducting a survey and writing a book on where to find the best and cheapest theatre seats in London. He thinks it a good idea but pointed out that it would have to be a long project because the cheapest seats are normally in the balcony and I am not physically up to tackling balcony staircases just yet. Joe suggested that I could wait downstairs while he watches the plays, tries the seats out and marks them out of ten. Trouble is, I couldn't stand around waiting for too long either and we both know who would have to pay for him to watch the plays!

Must stop now. Enjoy your trip to Ireland and thanks for the offer but don't worry about trying to bring me back a pot of gold. Although I wouldn't mind a freak leprechaun (a nice, tall dark one who will speak to me). That reminds me about one of Mr T's jokes about a frog… another time.

Lots of love, cheer up and happy hols.
B x

PS
Thanks for returning the original of my letter by the way but let's not get over the top about my 'future success' as a writer. Tell me you haven't had any acupuncture recently as you are showing some of the symptoms ha ha!

Chapter 6

Dialogue with Doris

Today, I went to see May's mother Doris, who is aged ninety and in hospital. May had been very good to me over recent months, making me laugh and bringing in talking books for me to listen to during the time that I was only able lie down. Doris had become quite a burden on May of late, refusing to take any medication for her arthritic legs and had worn her arms out pushing round the wheels on her wheelchair. May and countless other people had tried without success, to get her to agree to an electric one. Doris had also given up eating and I suspect, really just wanted to throw in the towel on life, but wasn't allowed to. She was in fact, such a character that no one wanted to let her go, least of all, her daughter, May. So, before setting off for the hospital I made my mind up to try to get Doris to agree to a few things; to accept an electric wheelchair, start eating properly and take a few painkillers to help her mobility. I had been warned that Doris might insult me as this otherwise sweet old lady was fiercely independent so I hoped I'd be up to the challenge.

On arriving at the hospital the first hurdle to overcome was gaining access to the ward. It was 8pm and dark in the open walkway. Eric had dropped me off by car. I stood outside the ward, pressing various security buttons for about ten minutes before anyone came to let me in. I had felt a bit vulnerable waiting outside in the dark, wearing my surgical collar and feeling very delicate due to more acupuncture jabs received in the neck the day before. Eventually, a male nurse answered the door buzzer and apologised for the delay. He explained that the security system was really intended to keep the patients in rather than any intruders out. I hoped for his own sake he hadn't shared this fact with Doris for it wasn't the kind of idea she would take to very well.

Doris was lying flat down flat on a railed-in bed at the end of a very long ward. I was surprised how well and happy she appeared and seemed delighted to see me. She greeted me like some long lost relative or, a recently found 'missing person'. Her face clouded over a bit though, when I presented her with the box of chocolates I had brought in. 'I don't like Ferrero Rocher,' she said. 'You eat them!' I suggested she hang on to the chocolates anyway. Perhaps she could offer them to other visitors, being all out of grapes. 'No,' she said. 'Ruby came in to see me today and she can't stand Ferrero Rocher either. Lots of people don't. You might as well take them home.' Deciding it would be wise to change the subject, I left the chocolates on the locker and leant over the bed to raise the subject of the electric wheelchair. As I did so, an alarm bell rang and two nurses suddenly appeared from nowhere to ask what had been the problem? Surprised at this, we assured them that everything was OK and they went away. I leant over the bed once more to converse with Doris and the same two nurses returned to the same spot like an apparition. Quite impressive service I thought, on behalf of the NHS. Between us we discovered that Doris must have inadvertently pressed down the bed alarm button as she turned towards me to try and hear what I was saying.

Obviously, brightening up a bit since the offending chocolate incident, Doris proceeded to make a dramatic introduction of me to loud gasps from the nurses: 'Look at this girl,' she insisted. 'She has had the most dreadful accident! A door fell on her neck!'

'No, Doris,' I said. 'Actually it was a Venetian blind and it hit me on the side of the head.'

'Oh no! Not one of those plastic ones?' said Doris.

'No, it was metal actually,' I replied.

'Oh my God!' she exclaimed, practically recoiling in her bed with horror. I attempted to play this all down a bit as I was feeling conspicuous in the collar and really embarrassed by the fuss my 'patient' was making especially in view of the fact that *she* were the one in a hospital bed. The nurses were obliged to commiserate with me, so made sympathetic tut tuts and headshakes on my behalf. Doris forced them to agree with her proclamation that I was 'absolutely marvellous', before they were allowed to leave us and return to the nurses' station and await another summons.

Taking advantage of being in Doris's good books, I broached the subject of the electric wheelchair. To my surprise, she requested that I 'look out for one' for her. I was really taken aback by this success and was just about to discuss her food intake when the alarm went off again and the same two nurses rushed on to the scene for the third time. Upon investigation it was discovered that the alarm cord had become wound around one of the chrome bars on Doris's bed. I had been resting on the bars to support my dodgy neck and shoulders, thereby pressing the rail down onto the buzzer. As one of the nurses attempted to untangle the alarm cord, Doris grabbed hold of it and refused to let it go, screeching out: 'Leave it where it is!' but calmed down after much assurance from us all that it wasn't going to be removed, just unwound.

Feeling more than a little weary by this time, I pushed on with my next task… the subject of Doris's eating habits. 'Do you know,' she said, 'I had mashed potato today and baked beans. I love baked beans don't you? I could eat them forever.' I suggested that she should have asked for another portion as beans are full of protein. 'Oh no,' said Doris, 'I have been well brought up; I know never to ask for more.' I said that the staff would be happy to feed her a lot more of them just to keep her eating and then Doris revealed that she also liked roast lamb. When I felt that she had been sufficiently coerced into a promise to eat more, I started on the subject of painkillers. I had a go at explaining how one pain could lead to another, hindering her movements and delay her discharge from hospital. Doris had never thought of this one before but had reservations about pill taking because you never knew what they would do to you.

'Ah,' I said. 'What about trying acupuncture?' and told her that it might be very good for straight forward pain relief (though I didn't seem to be a very good advertisement for it). When Doris realised that it was a 'natural' remedy, she said she would ask the doctor about it. I couldn't believe my success. Shortly after our conversation I decided to get out while I was winning and left for home, tired and happy that I had succeeded in what I had set out to do.

On the way home, Eric popped a note through May's door saying: MISSION ACCOMPLISHED!

That woman's confidence in me had been amazing. All I had to do now was go and inspect a few dozen wheelchairs. Did all this success have anything to do with that strange visit to the retreat centre or was it some type of energy escaping out of my acupuncture holes? In spite of my supposed ability to 'know truth', this time, I was unable to tell.

Wednesday morning found me back at the New Age Health Centre to see my osteopath. Dr Ling specialised mainly in acupuncture and I felt in need of a bit more manipulation from my osteopath, Heidi, who had known me for twenty years. I was still puzzled by what was wrong with me and despite looking up information about disc prolapses there seemed to be no hard and fast rules as to symptoms and recovery times etc. Dr Ling was very quiet and usually, noncommittal. He just did his stuff and said little, so I thought Heidi might clarify a few things as well as give me some neck traction. Heidi seemed a bit suspicious about all my acupuncture treatments and asked several questions about it. Maybe she couldn't understand why I had deserted her after all those years of devotion to be cracked and jumped on by her to be stabbed and prodded with needles by Dr Ling. I didn't know either. I sort of just got into it. Of course she was probably just being her usual professional self and wanting to understand what had been going on with my 'condition'. *Which one?* I asked myself. *The condition I was in physically or the odd stuff going on in my head?* I took the easy way out and didn't ask her. I did enquire though, about the 'iffy discs' and why no one could actually tell me much about them nor say when I'd recover. She cleared this up for me in a minute by saying that 'nobody really knew'. Well there's a relief I thought. It's not just me who is the thick one here. They're ALL daft. I asked her to describe in layman's terms what a slipped disc was. As far as I remember Heidi told me that the disc lay in some kind of jelly which, if it gets displaced, floats about a bit like the yolk of an egg and has to become stable again. There is also some runny liquid around too; some sort of acid which can seep somewhere. I lay there on the treatment couch staring at the ceiling and imagining a runny fried egg stuck to the back of my neck. Yep, I could make out the logic of that and it was the first clear picture received. I'd leave the question of the acid for now and bug some other medical expert with that question later. Meanwhile, I was happy with the fried egg bit and found it quite amusing, the thought of keeping my yolk straight, bit like a trapeze artist I suppose, without the vertigo. I wandered off home with this new information and dropped a line to the Chief Exec at work. It was stressing me so much being off work and not able to tell anyone when I'd be able to start back. I explained my physical state in as clear terms as possible (leaving out the fried egg bit). I cited some examples of my disability to keep him in the picture i.e. I was unable to stretch out and reach the shampoos in the chemist or sit for too long etc., etc. I put the letter in an envelope and took a walk to the post box. Being at home was definitely not doing me any good. I'm a great believer in work and think Voltaire was dead right all those years ago when he said we should all go and work in the garden except I'd rather go and boil an egg in the kitchen (and that IS saying something).

Dear Amanda,

Thanks for the phone message. I'm glad you're still talking to me. No I haven't considered taking H.R.T. I don't want any horse giving up its urine for my sake and the natural plant stuff I've heard about has side effects. Also, it stops you having hot flushes, and I've looked forward to those for years as they might enable me to leave my vests off. Of course my taste in vests is very particular. I must have walked miles over the years looking for sophisticated, glamorous black ones. My best purchase was a little 'all in one' number I found a few years ago and really thought I'd hit the jackpot. It was just like one of Jane Russell's. Jane was a really glam actress in the fifties. When I was a child, she and Joan of Arc were my idols along with Elizabeth Fry and Odette, the wartime intelligence agent. I had very mixed tastes in heroines... Jane always wore sexy black bisques in the spaghetti westerns she starred in and they looked a bit like my black lacy 'all in one'. It didn't serve me too well as a vest though, as the holes in the lace let in little drafts under my jumpers. So, the 'all in one' is now filed away in my 'just in case' drawer along with my tiny, silk knickers – all reserved for when I go on a diet and start to receive hot flushes.

I think I might have experienced one of those while at dinner in Portugal last year. At the time I put it all down to climate change. I began to suspect there might be some other explanation for the sudden rise in temperature after I'd asked everyone around me whether they could feel it and discovered that it only applied to me. When the reason for this hit me I almost died of embarrassment. Another occasion when I wished I'd been able to keep my big mouth shut.

Amanda, I've just heard about an organisation called 'FALS'. It stands for 'Find another Life'. It's surprising anyone could find the energy for it, as one seems enough to cope with. I'm not qualified to join at the moment not being a divorcee. Anyway, I watched a TV programme about this finding another life business. Two women in Sussex started up a support group apparently. I noticed they had the same sort of looks as women I'd seen at a Buddy Greco concert some years ago; middle-aged groupies with top layered 'big hair' and long straggly bits hanging down. That cured me of wanting shoulder length hair and made me have mine cut off to avoid any similarity. Mind you, those two 'FALS' women did look pretty well preserved plus, there was a strong sparkle of independence about them. Several of the newer club members appearing rather worn and wane, as though beaten down by domesticity and boredom. Maybe club meetings and a few trips away will do the trick for them. I might write in and suggest a 'just in case' drawer for their holidays.

Goodbye for now,
B x

Chapter 7

The Strange Case of Dr Zani

Made three visits to the FPA clinic this week before finally getting there for the correct appointment time. Another set of occasions when my mind seemed to be on another planet; I managed to get all the appointment times mixed up. Feeling also a need to get away from the house for a spell, I moved in with my sister for a short break then spent a few days with my niece Millie and family. I had left home temporarily to try and forget all those miserable winter months spent lying on my back (trying to put my discs back in line of course). I'd recently suffered another ten-day chronic pain flare up and this sparked of depression. So, I took off for the delights of SE6 and after a few days felt somewhat 'back in the world' again, but still unable to shake off the bleak moods which had overtaken me. This was the reason for not being able to concentrate or get my appointments right. The next being due with the FPA clinic and my appointment with Dr Zani. As I was no longer the chatty patient he had known for twenty years, Dr Z was curious to know what was the matter. In a voice I hardly recognised as my own, I filled him in on a few details of the previous seven months and my injury. He listened intently then glanced at my notes and said, 'Good God! It's three years since you've been here for a new diaphragm.'

'Is it?' I said. 'Doesn't time fly?' Dr Z gave me a quizzical look so I told him that to be honest the thing didn't get as much use as it had in the past. 'Anyway,' I said, 'I have been a bit disabled since last winter and naturally, it has affected my relationship with my husband.' We hadn't been communicating very well on several levels actually.

This confession seemed to give Dr Zani the inspiration to launch into a discussion on his own relationship with his wife. 'Nobody's perfect,' he said. 'Take me for example, I'm not perfect.' He seemed to expect me to disagree with him, which I wouldn't have done. To me, he was just another middle-aged man, who, to be polite, cut rather a chubby figure (especially around the stomach and belt department). As though to give me a further opportunity to disagree with him, Dr Zani emphasised again that he wasn't perfect. I sat in silence while he went on to tell me how he had to suffer numerous visits to M & S with Mrs Zani (and presumably his cheque card), which he secretly hated. Dr Z's idea on how to sort out communication problems between husband and wife took me somewhat by surprise when he suggested, rather animatedly, that Eric and I go off to the Amazon and zip ourselves up in a tent! I began to wonder whether the good doctor ought to be zipped up in a straitjacket for safety sake because he appeared to be getting himself over excited about 'the cure'. I wondered if Mrs Z ought to be warned off taking her husband around M & S as I imagined that he probably spent his time staring at the ladies' lingerie section while she was queuing up with her purchases and it was obviously not doing him any good. Well, that was one problem we didn't have in our house. I rarely shopped with my husband at all. You need something – go and buy it. He needs something – he goes to buy it. Quite straight forward really and that's the way Eric liked to be – no complications.

I really upset E one evening when he was watching one of his favourite old western films on TV. I asked if he had heard that the hero – his favourite actor now deceased – may have been into cross dressing. Eric stood up, switched off the TV and proclaimed, 'Well, that's it. My faith in humanity has just been completely shattered,' and cleared off to bed. I thought that a very profound statement for him to make while there was a film playing (though I didn't notice whether it had actually finished or not). Anyway, that's the sort of life he likes to have; clear, straightforward and no complications to think about. On the plus side, he is compassionate and kind and doesn't approve of satire or any joke that insults others, which he sees as the lowest form of wit. I had always admired Eric for knowing exactly what he did and didn't like and quietly standing by what he thought. Maybe Dr Zani was right after all though; life was a bit flat between us, but I think camping in the Amazon could be a hazardous place for someone with iffy discs in her neck and a fear of spiders.

I thanked Dr Zani for his advice but said that I wasn't too sure about the Amazon at this time of year. He said not to worry, that I could go and chat to him any time I wanted and without an appointment too. Before I left, Dr Z had a go at using his counselling skills by trying to get me to cry, and without success I might add, so I bade him goodbye and walked out. He had been right about one thing, I did feel like crying but had given myself plenty of practise at learning how not to do it. Dr Z was obviously not as good a counsellor as he thought. All my clients at work seemed to crack up and let it all out in front of me whatever I said. Dr Zani had made one vital mistake in his counselling method: never reveal your own stuff. It makes the client feel their needs are secondary. That is why I was left feeling I ought to go back and talk to him again to give him the chance to get the M & S and the ladies' lingerie stuff of his chest. On second thoughts, perhaps not such a good idea.

Before my next visit to the 'Buddhist doctor', I called in to see my pal Julia from whom he had been recommended. It was intended to be just a quick visit and short chat but J insisted on pouring an Arnica tablet down my throat before I left because it would 'do me good'. I wasn't allowed to touch the pill with my fingers for fear of contamination and reducing its efficacy. Her therapeutic accomplice, Emily, always distributes these to accident victims apparently. I think Julia couldn't wait for a road accident victim to play doctor so someone who had suffered a venetian blind accident would have to do instead. I could see J's point. After all, Emily's flat was a ground floor one. Julia, living in a third floor flat would not have the same immediate access to accident victims. I must admit that when Julia opened her medicine cabinet I was rather surprised at its contents because she probably had enough homeopathic remedies to start her own business. Julia also has a doctor's manner about her. She is kind yet brusque, sometimes and is persistent in telling you what to do until you finally do it. I expect she picked this up from years of teaching English to overseas doctors. I wouldn't be surprised if she were also able to teach them a bit about medicine too. Either way, I bet it wouldn't stop her trying if she had a mind too! I could see that it might be necessary to get myself into alternative medicine mode since I had been to one of their meetings and geared myself up to it. Everything seemed a bit hasty though as I still found myself half in the world of orthodox medicine for the time being. It was a bit like giving yourself up to Jesus before the formal baptism. Anyway, later that day I went for the needle treatment so I guess this was another forward step towards my initiation into the 'alternative world'.

Arriving at the musculoskeletal clinic I didn't feel up to much that day and probably had a bad cold or virus starting. After a few minutes Dr L came to collect me, and I sat down in silence while he studied an arrowed diagram of my physique. I was then invited to give him a quick rundown of the previous three weeks. This I did (leaving out the bits about my mother of course) but sticking to my latest symptoms; an aching shoulder and leg plus a stiff back. After being acupunctured several times in the neck, I was asked to lie down on my front on the treatment table. I achieved this with some difficulty as the table was too high for me to ascend easily, probably adjusted correctly to avoid the good Dr getting back strain. As he must be about six feet tall and I am five feet three and three quarters there was bound to be some discrepancy affecting the ease at which I could be accommodated. Clambering on to the table and clutching the sides I dragged and slid myself to the top, like a beached whale making its way up the sand. I then had to stick my face into a specially designed hole in the table that allowed a terrific view of the Marley tiled floor below. In order to sort out the pain in my leg, I was needled several times in the right hip. Imagine my embarrassment when Dr L asked me whether I kept a hot water bottle there. I couldn't believe it, was nothing sacred? I felt like a five-year-old, who was forced to admit that she still had a dummy. Dr L helpfully informed me that I had some heat marks on my right hip that would go away if I stopped lying on the bottle, but if I continued using the water bottle at that temperature my skin would become discoloured. Believe me, I thought, where I keep that bottle no one is likely to get a view of those spots. Even Eric would need to put his glasses on in the unlikely event that he might want to study them. All this healthy stuff gets a bit much sometimes, no tobacco, no alcohol and now, no hot water bottle. It was just handy that I didn't have to remove my tights and reveal the fake tan on my chubby legs. Is there anyone who doesn't think orange cellulite is much more preferable to white? Probably Dr Ling, I doubt he would approve of anything as 'unnatural' or potentially harmful as 'Tanfastic' tan cream. Admittedly, it does have a strange odour, which is why I have to spray my legs with Chanel after the cream dries off. Quite an expensive day if you look at Dr Ling's medical fees and my train fares (not to mention the Chanel squirts for the legs). I did get my money's worth that day though. Apart from the skin advice and needling I was covered with a white sheet and given some Osteopathic bone crunching to finish the proceedings. How I had the energy to get home that day and crawl into bed for a snooze I shall never know.

Chapter 8

You Can't Choose Your Family

My cousin Jake (Sonny), now a middle-aged wannabe society drop out, is a reformed character since he got a proper full-time job. Well, full time for him – twenty-eight hours a week and a lot of tea. I went to see him at his office the other day to elicit his help for when I re-start my management project. (Elicit is in my vocabulary a lot since I did that CELTA course.) Sonny was most accommodating; it's amazing what a bit of adversity does in life. You see his long-term partner left him a few years ago because she was sick of paying the mortgage. That was in the days when Sonny was called Jake and did a bit of freelance photography, a bit of guitar playing and the occasional building job. Sonny alias Jake takes a lot of understanding because he doesn't agree with society, well most of it anyway, so doesn't really want to conform and join in. Actually, I agree with him entirely because I feel as if I'm only in it by the skin of my teeth but it's like a sort of compulsory club where you have to join in or you'll never get your badge or afford to eat a proper dinner. I've had a lot of respect for Jake since he reverted to his real name of Sonny. It took a lot of doing for someone like him like him because working with college students meant that most of them were Jake types too. Because of his new job, he was forced to choose an identity for himself, hence his rehabilitation. Sonny now looks like Lenin, with a goatee beard and round glasses, wears 'proper' clothes to work and makes a lot of tea. Although, he still sniffs a lot and sighs 'oh dear' as though it's all too much effort, but I always knew he had it in him only he didn't want anyone to see. His new career venture seems a bit like someone 'coming out' – a big surprise to everyone.

In spite of all this I know Sonny would rather be seen as Jake underneath by what he said to me the other evening. He had called in on his way to the pub to 'correct' something I'd written up (I forgot to say he graduated two years ago, carries the title of historian and is now a trained teacher). After delivering me a short lecture on something or other standing with his hands in his pockets and wearing his Lenin glasses, he offered to pass on a late Xmas present to my six-year-old nephew. As S left the house and I watched him struggle down the driveway with the big box, I called out, 'Thanks' and remarked how tough it was becoming a Samaritan.

'Yeah,' he called back over his shoulder, 'I think I'll go back to being a piss artist!' I'm not sure what one of those is but it sounds like a profession he might be qualified to take up. There's no hope for some people is there? I don't like his language but love him just the same and why I'll never know. He's just openly obnoxious with an odd tinge of humanity about him. My mother is one of his fans and loves recalling the time, that four-year-old Sonny (alias Jake but aka Dennis the Menace) was found dragging a raw leg of lamb (intended for the Sunday roast) around our garden on a piece of string. Apparently, his Mum, Aunt Rose, rinsed it and put it back in my mother's fridge where it belonged but didn't tell my mother any of this until years after we had eaten it.

Talking of Mum, I had to accompany her on another of her many hospital visits last week. We took a cab to the hospital then made our way into 'Outpatients'. We had the usual performance of her being unable to walk, carry her stick and carrier bags and at the same time hang on to my 'good' arm, which always seemed to end up being on her 'wrong' side. We circled each other a few times before getting it right and into a uniform pace then along on to suite four. On the noticeboard at reception, I had read the name of my surgeon cousin, David, who I had come across a few times in the course of his occupation and my ailments. A stroke of luck I thought, maybe I could catch up with him and arrange to get a fourth opinion on my scans and X-rays? As it happened, David made the mistake of nipping out of his consulting room to go to the loo while M was being weighed. On his way back from the loo, I discreetly stuck out my surgically collared neck and smiled at him. He stopped and asked me what had happened. I explained the neck business etc. and he was about to give me what I hoped was a quick diagnosis when M arrived from the weighing room, spotted him and started going on about all our old relatives (most of whom David and I had never met). How did she always manage to do it? – put her foot or, stick her bags in the wrong place at the wrong time! Once she had taken over the conversation that was the end of my 'would be' diagnosis. After ten minutes of talking with my mother, David said he had better get back to his clinic. Before he left, D happily accepted my invitation to meet up with all the family at my house. (This will probably be next year sometime as I am planning on us knocking down a few walls and getting in some new furniture before that event.)

At last it was time for Mum to see her consultant who couldn't find anything wrong with her and announced that she was 'in good nick'. Not to be deterred, M asked another couple of dozen questions and then requested to ask one more (about holidays of all things). *Oh no*, I thought, she's *going to ask about one of those social services holidays* (and I knew who would have to go with her!). Surprisingly, though, M asked if she were fit enough to fly abroad? When, 'Oh no, that means I will have to go with her and I'M not fit enough,' escaped my lips, the Doc smiled and apologised for saying the wrong thing. The consultation over, I took a few deep breaths to relax the tension in my neck before frog marching M down to the main reception to wait for a cab home.

We watched as several cabs came and Mum peering in suspiciously at all the drivers not immediately calling out the names of the pre-booked passengers. In Mum's opinion, doctors were the only men you could trust. One chap who had come to pick up his wife looked very suspicious indeed to Mum. She'd thought he was a cab driver and instructed me not to get into the car because he resembled the wife beater in the Tina Turner film seen on TV the previous Sunday. No wonder I am neurotic!

The following week saw me back at the local hospital once more, this time to visit my nephew Mike (our whole family practically live there). Eric and I walked gingerly into Mike's ward feeling quite worried as he had been admitted a few days earlier with a suspected ulcer. Apparently, Mike had been in quite a bad way when admitted to emergency, with strange stomach pains. We were not sure how he might be feeling about having a visit but we soon found out. A nurse indicated to us the appropriate bed which was empty, and said that our patient had 'probably gone for a walk'. E and I decided to go and fetch a cup of tea from the canteen then return to the ward and wait for Mike. On the way there, I thought I could perceive the long-legged strides of my nephew in the distance, seemingly devoid of any pain, wearing blue striped pyjama bottoms, a frayed tee shirt with 'Africa 91' spelled out in large letters on the back. He was carrying a newspaper under his arm and licking an ice cream. When we managed to catch up with him, M acted as though it were an everyday occurrence to take a ride in an ambulance and charge through the high street with a blue light flashing. He thanked us for coming, said he was fine now then wandered off still licking his ice cream cone. Without knowing he wanted us to or not, we followed Mike back to the ward for a short conversation with him before setting off for home leaving our nephew to enjoy his ice cream, newspaper and being 'poorly'. One satisfied patient, I'd say.

Oddities seem to run in our family, Eric says it all comes from my side of the family (he may be right of course but don't tell my mother), things are bad enough. This trait was brought to mind when I received a recent parcel from son Peter, currently working in Hong Kong. I was thrilled to discover inside it an authentic, special Chinese teapot on a stand which would look just fine in my cabinet, because it certainly wasn't big enough to supply tea to any one person in my family! I had asked Peter for a small piece of Jade as a present from China but was gently assured that anything of a significant size would be rather too expensive. So, I would satisfy myself with the teapot. After all, we only had about three in the kitchen already but they were all English and somewhat larger. I soon discovered that my new gift really was meant for pouring tea when I came across the instructions for use. This prompted a letter…

Dear Peter,
Thank you for the kind thoughts and teapot, very nice indeed. However, I am thinking of dropping a line to The Best Tea House Co. Ltd about their instructions. I can't impress my friends with real China tea because the instructions on how to make it give me a headache and would make most people crack up laughing. Also, I don't understand the bit about boiling the tea pot for two hours. Julia says it is probably to get all the poison out of the clay. But, you wouldn't send your Mummy a poisoned teapot would you? Anyway, I shall write off and see what they say about my list of questions as the logic was probably lost in translation. Thought I'd tell you though, that I received a reply from our MP Brenda Wicks about the complaints I made concerning your proxy voting form and the instructions for completion which almost beat the directions for using your teapot – clear as mud! She replied to say that she is taking my complaint further (but

doesn't know I have already done that and contacted the Home Office). Maybe I won't say anything about my efforts as MPs like to be seen doing something useful just before an election. Brenda Wicks also thinks we should get the Plain English Campaign to take a look at the form and I might get her to send a copy of the teapot instructions to for a second opinion too! By the way, Cara suggested you might like to send me some catalogues from one or two of the shops in Hong Kong so that I can choose a present for myself. Be nice to have a treat and, as I mentioned before: maybe a tiny, jade, figurine, or even a Suzy Wong dress? Since my Chinese acupuncture I have been feeling very oriental in spirit but seem to lack the adornments that go with it!

Please let Dad know what you want him to cook for Alex to bring out to you when he visits. It was Alex's own idea. He seems to think you might appreciate a bit of home cooking. I didn't like to tell him how insulting you have always been about me burning things as he seems such a polite lad and I am sure he would be really embarrassed to think he had touched on a sore point. So, I thought something made by Dad might be a better idea. The trouble is, Dad can only really make soup, a bit of a leak risk I should have thought for carrying to Hong Kong. So, on second thought how about a nice bit of Sainsbury's Battenberg cake? It always used to put you in a good mood and it's a fair exchange for a bit of green Jade isn't it (hint hint).

Forgot two important pieces of news; Robert and Frances had a baby boy last week and you need to write me something funny if you want to be in 'The Book'. Also, the manager of the Curry Garden sends his regards to you and was most interested to learn about your stay in HK. I suggested he might like to pay you a visit (hope you don't mind) and you had better hurry up and hire out that junk you were talking about because cousin Sonny wants to come out for a holiday too. I can't see that your one-bedroom flat in Sing Woo Road will be big enough if Alex, Sonny and the Indian visitors all turn up at once. Also, I found out that the Curry Garden manager has a wife and three children. Sorry about that, son, I spoke before I thought about how you might accommodate all of them. I am sure you will manage though dear.

Love from us at home,
Mum x

Shortly after I had written to Peter, his old friend Andy popped in to see us and I showed him my present from Hong Kong. Andy was clearly, unimpressed by my dinky little ceremonial teapot and said it wouldn't prove very useful in my house with the rate that we consumed tea and that Peter would have been better advised to send me an urn. He wasn't at all complementary about Peter's choice in gifts saying that he would put my tea pot on a par with the present he'd received from Hong Kong too. 'An ornament of two little fat kids holding up a turnip.' I defended my son and accused Andy of just not appreciating Peter's oriental taste. Later that day, P rang to check I had received the teapot all in one piece as he'd dropped the package on the way to the post office! I told him Andy thought the pot was not big enough for the amount of beverage served in our house. P apologised but said as he couldn't afford the postage for an urn we would just have to make do with a spoonful of tea each!

While in the mood I wrote another letter...

Hi there Mrs Green,

Guess what, Amanda? I am going to have to get a 'pusher' (shopping basket on wheels) as Eric now has a bad back which makes him walk sideways like a crab. He couldn't collect my medical certificate from the doctor, so I went for it. I tried to carry a few things back from the shops but had to stop and buy myself a shopper in the 'Sell You Anything' store at Leonardgate. Very useful, the pusher except I couldn't push it much because of my arm. BUT, I have discovered an additional use for the disabled neck collar. It stops you getting run over! Even rowdy, rough looking, drivers in cars with loud music blaring, sometimes stop for you even if you are crossing on an amber light. There's an elderly lady around here who wears a surgical collar. She rushes across the road at the traffic lights carrying a Zimmer frame. I say carrying, because I have never actually seen her using it though I have watched her with curiosity for weeks. It's as though she can't trust the cars to stop and reserves all her energy to make a quick dash across the road and then slows down to a halt when she reaches the other side. Perhaps she is vulnerable in the neck and spine department so hurries across the road when it is clear because she can't rotate her head to look at for traffic but is afraid of falling over, hence the use of frame and collar. I think everyone over fifty should wear one for walking out; it might cut down on the road accident rate.

Another visit to the GP again this morning for painkillers. Life is getting really expensive having to pay for drugs, minicabs and Dr Ling's fees. I met my next door neighbours, Lucas and Hetty in the waiting room, what a coincidence! Lucas and I loitered by the door as the waiting room was full up with people coughing and spluttering all over the place, some of them obviously going down with flu. As Hetty sat herself down in what appeared to be the flu section, I asked Lucas if he thought Hetty had it too, but L said she was only there for a blood pressure test. I panicked to see H sitting there amongst all the germs in that section of the room. Lucas said Hetty was only sitting there to keep Mr Wilson Company as he did have FLU! I couldn't see the sense in Hetty risking a seat there even if Mr W was a lone widower.

Interestingly, Lucas told me that even though he and Hetty had lived in the same house for over thirty-five years he had a different doctor from her. L thought a lot of time and money was wasted treating people suffering from viruses with antibiotics. His doctor had given him a sputum test once and his medication worked marvellously because the sputum test enabled the GP to prescribe an antibiotic with greater accuracy. We both thought it made a lot of sense though the NHS would be unlikely to adopt the idea in all cases due to the cost of testing. I looked around me and it did seem rather ridiculous. All those people sitting about in the waiting room, infecting each other, some even waiting for first or repeat prescriptions for possibly the wrong medication! I was glad to have stocked myself up on vitamin C at home. If I had to put up with flu as well as everything else it would have been the final straw. Already feeling depressed, I told Dr B so when directed in to see him. Speaking in a lowered voice, as though letting him into a big secret I told Dr B how 'down' I had been. God knows why I should have felt ashamed of feeling that way. It wasn't really surprising under the circumstances. When I admitted to him that at times I felt like ending it all, Dr B was very sympathetic but told me that if that was what I really intended he wouldn't be able to stop me. Very subtle this last statement because its simple logic left me puzzling to such a degree that I decided to put off this irreversible act until I really needed it like when I develop arthritis in a few years' time. You see I really missed the dancing and the parties we used to have on New Year's Eve. Our house was normally full to over brimming on 31 December. This last one I had to spend lying down on the sofa, grateful to have been able to have the choice of sitting up for a while. Yes, I missed the noise as well as the dreaded tobacco smoke.

I went home armed with a prescription, another medical certificate for work and a resolve not to do myself in until absolutely necessary.

Amanda, it is about time you rang, or, wrote and made me laugh! Just remembered, two things I want to ask you. Did you get my message on the answerphone about avoiding Red Kooga Ginseng at the moment? Stick to the Siberian stuff but taking vitamin C with it dilutes its strength. Also, can you give me any ideas on how Eric can make frozen spinach interesting? I need it for my calcium levels (I'm cutting down on the milk for slimming purposes). Thanks very much.
Take care!
Love,
B x

Chapter 9

A Fourth Treatment

Dr Ling was in a suspiciously jocular mood today and dressed in civvies (I mean minus his white coat). Noticeably, he had on a deep blue shirt and yellow patterned tie that matched his eyes beautifully. The shirt I mean, not the tie. I'd never noticed he had coloured eyes before. Usually, everything about him seemed to just blend in with the stiff white coat. Maybe he had been visiting a consultant too; a colour consultant who'd advised him to lay off white. My friend Eileen is one of those. I found out how useful she was one day when everyone in the office suspected me of having a dose of flu or being in a bad mood. I flew into Eileen's office and asked her what was wrong with the way I looked. Eileen studied me for a few minutes before announcing her diagnosis: 'It's that shirt,' she said. 'It's the wrong shade of cream for you. The silk reflects badly on your skin and makes you look peaky. Get rid of it!' Perhaps someone told Dr Ling that about his white coat as he was definitely 'a blue boy' as my mother-in-law used to say. Also, I didn't really think that particular white coat suited a man of his position. It reminded me of those worn by supermarket butcher's staff (though to be fair they usually topped the coats off with white trilby hats too). As Dr Ling wasn't a surgeon, I hoped there was no connection between him and butchery but you never can tell can you? Anyway, something had definitely put him in a good mood because he actually spoke a few words and made some light-hearted comments about not being able to find me 'hiding' in the waiting room and wondered if the summer weather suited me. Stunned by the unusual circumstance that he was leading the conversation and not me the fact rendered me (practically) speechless for a change. I wondered why Dr

Ling was being so pleasant and figured there could be one of only two reasons for this. Either he was trying to cheer me up after receiving another bulletin from his informant Emily (via Julia), about the time I had freaked out, left home and gone to stay with my sister, or he was going on holiday again. The latter would mean that he'd be spared a few weeks away from me and my interminable pain stricken notes. Yes, it all added up. He was attired in his holiday clothes and dreaming of Africa. I say this, because Dr L looked like a man who went to Africa for his holidays; tall, in charge and probably not afraid of spiders. I suppose he could afford it with all that private needling he did. Yes, definitely not the type to sit in Lunn Poly trying to locate the best out of season bargain for a week abroad. Just think, my misfortune had probably paid for about two days of his exotic holiday. I couldn't begrudge him though. Dr L deserved it for putting up with patients like me (assuming there were any others like me).

I tried to re-negotiate my treatment this time and said I felt the need of manipulation rather than acupuncture. Maybe traction treatment I suggested? The reason for this was that I was now on anti-depressants and not sure if people ought to have acupuncture whilst on them. I didn't want to let on to Dr Ling about them because it wasn't a 'natural' remedy and felt that I was letting the side down. Depression was the reason I had gone to stay with my sister and have a change of environment. Dr Ling still recommended the needle treatment and said I had some deep tissue damage and that the only way to get to it was to needle me. I finally had to own up, whispered the name of the antidepressant and awaited a telling off. What would my punishment be I wondered? I didn't wait long to find out. 'Oh! Acupuncture works very well with antidepressants,' he announced so enthusiastically that the patients in the waiting room must have heard. Well, what a surprise. Wouldn't you just know it? *Stab* went the needles, straight into my neck. *Take that*, they seemed to be telling me. As he manipulated the needles to find the most painful spot he began to ask some questions. Always a bad time to speak to me as I never could concentrate on two things at once (his words and the direction of the needles). 'Sleeping well?' he barked at me as though I were deaf. What was up with him, I do not know. He seemed determined to let everyone outside that room know my business. Maybe, he needed his ears syringed and didn't realise how loud he was speaking. Anyway, when Dr L announced. 'That's it.' I asked if I could have some traction. I thought I might as well get my money's worth as he was going on holiday and this was to be my last treatment for a while. He graciously agreed to give me 'a little tug' and started to move my neck from side to side first (I'd forgotten that bit). I recognised the rhythmical movement of this and knew what was coming next!

'Oh no!' I said. 'I hate this one!'

'Deep breath in, deep breath out, good!' he barked at me. 'Good!' he said again as he flung my neck about to the left. The next trick took me somewhat by surprise as he tugged my neck gently at first, then pulled me along what felt like the whole length of the couch! How anyone could heave a dead weight of ten and a half stone at that angle without slipping a disc or falling over backwards was beyond my imagination (even mine). I have given this a lot of thought since then and have come up with a very logical explanation for his success. Maybe, there were two metal stirrups set into the floor underneath the couch into which he slipped his feet. This would explain how Dr Ling had been able to keep his balance when dispensing 'little tugs'. Quite remarkable really, I was full of admiration as this wasn't the kind of treatment my osteopath had ever done but maybe she didn't have the same equipment under her couch. I made a note to check it out in my Alternative Therapy book (the one that's overdue at the library). My books were usually overdue at the library because I could only read lying down and then usually dropped off to sleep. Consequently, a book often took a long time to get through.

Retiring to the consulting room where Dr L was busily working away at his notes, I said goodbye quietly so as not to disturb him. As usual, he made no reply, concentrating heavily on his work maybe, or being just plain rude? I was never quite sure. Could I tell a consultant he was ill-mannered without running the risk of not having treatment at all or of receiving an extra spiteful one for complaining? Decision made, button my mouth. I had to hand it to him though, Dr L was right about the good mix of pills and needles. Things felt good, and I found myself back on automatic pilot again like after the last treatment. However, this time I was even walking in the right direction! On reaching the railway station I felt very proud of myself for only nearly getting run over by a car once instead of the usual twice. That's why it is worth going to a private consultant. He knew exactly what he was talking about; it was worth every penny of those little tugs and I even lived to tell the tale.

Chapter 10

Local Business

Monday found me going to photocopy my medical certificates and a few notes to send in to work. Mrs Singh, the lady who ran the local sweet shop and post office with her husband, was seated elegantly on a high wooden stool dressed in a flowing red sari. From this vantage point, she was able to observe the antics of any less than honest customers (namely the after school crowd) which time it was heading towards now. I had known Mr and Mrs Singh since my children were little, about twenty-five years in fact but one rarely got a peep out of them unless it was to quote me prices. They were a quiet couple and Mr Singh always looked miserable. He served behind the post office counter so it wasn't surprising. In my experience post office staff are often grumpy. It must be come from filling in all those boring forms. Maybe he was fed up with meeting old folk, poor people on benefit and kids screaming for sweets while their Mums queued up for the family allowance. Anyway, Mr Singh was grumpy for some reason or another and I'd often wondered why he always kept his right hand hidden, in his pocket. I used to think it was something to do with his culture or religion (but thought that applied to the left hand?). This puzzled me for years until I heard that poor Mr Singh had lost his hand in an accident and had a metal hook on the end of his right arm. I never met anyone who had actually seen it but that was the rumour.

As I said, despite all the years we had known each other, Mrs Singh and I rarely got into conversation. Today was to be the exception. As I waited for a young man to finish photocopying a pile of documents, Mrs Singh started to reminisce on how many years had gone by since we had last met and to ask about my 'children'. I should have known that her object was to tell me all about the law course her son on the photocopier was doing. It was all very interesting up until the point she began saying to me that we were older than we realised, weren't we, and then launched into a history of her HRT problems. *Speak for yourself*, I thought. As far as I was concerned, if my eighty-nine-year-old mother still considered herself middle aged I could easily forget a couple of decades on an optimistic day. At last, it was my turn and I got to use the copier. Relief turned to vexation as I witnessed my photocopied sheets come flying off the machine as there was no paper tray fixed on to the machine to collect them. I hadn't noticed this problem when Singh junior had been using it. He must have been efficiently grabbing each sheet as it was processed. I had to keep stooping and picking mine up of the floor. Not the best thing for a shaky neck (it wasn't a good day from this aspect). I eventually got around to stuffing the papers into an envelope only to find that the moistened gum on the envelope wouldn't stick. Without thinking too much about it, I took the stuffed envelope over to Mrs Singh and asked her if she would oblige by sitting on it for a few minutes to weigh the contents down and help the glue to stick. I didn't think to add that I always did this with envelopes to be on the safe side. The expression on Mrs Singh's face at this question was one that I had never seen before, the surprise evidently causing her to almost fall of her stall. When I explained the reason for my request she stared at me eagle eyed; obviously startled at the suggested action. I was even more startled when, without a word, she handed me some sellotape and scissors. I had never known Mrs Singh to be generous with anything before. I should have thought that sitting on my envelope would have been less expensive for the business. In view of this I took her gesture as a sign of friendship and camaraderie as we were obviously both in the same age group; a fact which seemed to provide some comfort to her rather sombre mood of reminiscence.

I resolved not to bother Mrs Singh about anything for a while and crossed the road to see Mr Gobi my friendly, local pharmacist, would be chief medical adviser and part-time comedian. Mr G was sitting with his leg up on the counter looking bored. He enquired how I was. I asked him for some co-codamol pills 'off prescription', and a receipt to go with them. 'What do you want a receipt for?' he said. 'It's a free country... you can buy what you like. What's the world coming to?' Either my request had thrown Mr G into a fit of apoplexy or he was joking. I could never really tell. I explained why the prescription was needed and jokingly, asked whether he were 'on drugs'.

'I'm always on drugs,' he said. I suppose it's difficult to resist temptation when you are a pharmacist though his eyes looked alright to me. Quite nice eyes really for a medical type person (I was into eyes of late). My fascination used to be for people with pleasant voices. Years ago it was for those who wore sunglasses on their heads until it became common practise. I had recently become more interested in feet since having my corns done regularly at the chiropodist. Eric said that being off sick for a long time I might as well get everything fixed. So I stated with the feet and ended up at the FPA but that was another story. Having an increased understanding of the chiropody profession was cause for thought. If I could combine my interest in languages with my interest in feet I might, one day, become a bilingual podiatrist! That's the trouble with being a careers adviser, you always want to do somebody else's job. All my colleagues are the same. I am even planning what work to do on retirement. All presuming I can GET back to work!

Before taking leave of Mr Gobi, I expressed surprise that he was still open even though it was past his normal lunchtime. Mr G said that he was 'getting soft', that he never used to care whether anyone needed a prescription between 1 and 2pm, but now it worried him. We were interrupted just then by one of Mr Gobi's white turbaned pals who had kindly dropped in to take his lunch order: 'I'd like a cod and chips please,' said Mr G. No sooner had he placed this order with the kindly Sikh than in came another two customers. At this point I thought I had better raise my next query in case we ran out of time. I told Mr G that I thought the last lot of prescription pills I had been issued with might have had a counter reaction with my corn plasters and instigated pains in my big toe. As I started to tell him about it he rudely interrupted me with: 'Go on then, explain what happened, I could do with a laugh, I've not had one all day.' I explained that I had read something on the corn plaster packet about certain antibiotics having adverse reactions with a substance on the plaster and that I had suffered pains in two big toes after my last course of antibiotics. Mr G took hold of the corn plaster packet and read out the warning on the side. The medicine it named on the pack was nothing like the one I had been taking and I had clearly misread the warning (didn't tell him I had lost my reading glasses). I apologised and felt my face flush with embarrassment as this little interlude had informed a shop full of people not only that I had bad feet but in addition, I was probably suspected of being illiterate or partially sighted with dubious mental faculties. Apologising again for wasting his time, I shot off the premises before Mr G could get everyone laughing at me as well as himself.

Later that week I went for a chat with Dr B and thought I would give him the lowdown on my latest discovery about acupuncture and the release of serotonin in the brain. Dr B seemed very interested but when he said, 'Actually, you are talking to a complete ignoramus here,' I corrected him on this and said that actually, he was the one talking to an ignoramus and could he help me out with the bit I had read about electrical impulses and neurons, as I thought he probably understood more about neurons than I did. Dr B let his humility slip for a minute by revealing his very wide knowledge and explaining very simply in terms I could understand how it all worked. I could see that I had taken him back to his student days and probably to a professor whom I was unlikely to come In contact with having never studied at Oxford. I couldn't deny that my uncompleted modular course at UEL wasn't much of a comparison with an Oxbridge medical degree. Despite such professional setbacks, I had the impression that unless Professor X had any findings to reveal regarding the invalidity of acupuncture, it was OK by Dr B. It may be a good idea to get the chap's full name and ask my librarian friend May B to find out what she could about his views on acupuncture. Dr B might find it interesting too and it could save him the time of looking it all up. I am sure our conversations have sparked some more interest in the area of complementary medicine.

Before leaving, I made a mental note to check the bit about serotonin with Dr Ling next time we met.

Hi Amanda,

How are you? Any happier these days? You haven't said anything about my George Melly CD or the Tyrolean dance music I sent so, I guess they didn't work for you. Well, today they are not working for me either, because I AM REALLY FED UP BEING SO FAT and sick of drinking black coffee and eating carrots. I can't do any exercise (apart from the ones for my neck and shoulders) and I'm like a big white blob of lard only lard is less wobbly. I keep moving the scales to different parts of the house to try and get a lower reading. In one room I am 10 stone 13 pounds, and in another, 11 stone 2 pounds. Eric was only 11 stone when we married and he is six feet tall!

Pretty soon I shall have to resort to wearing Kaftans on a regular basis.

If I do manage to lose weight do you think I should try and keep myself motivated by writing a slimming book? Or maybe invest in a self-hypnosis CD and try to think myself slim. By the way, dearly beloved has tried to cheer me up by saying that I haven't got a bad figure then ruining the whole effect by adding the usual 'for your age'. I didn't find that comment very helpful. Firstly, he wears glasses, secondly, as long as I go in and out at the right places I've noticed he is not too choosey, and thirdly, as he is now fat as well, how reliable is that judgement?

There is also a fatty hump on the back of my neck which, may, or may not go according to what the doctor feels like telling me on the day AND that's not the only hump I've got today.

Please send a get slim message for encouragement.

Yours,
B x

Chapter 11

Medics – Another Breed

I was really happy last week after receiving two birthday presents through the post and only two weeks late! One was a lovely bag from Amanda and the other, a handmade beaded necklace from my friend's seven-year-old daughter Lisa in Vienna. I was thrilled to think she had made it for me and quickly tried it on. As I admired it on in the mirror I noticed my throat and neck begin to ache. This neck trouble was a never ending saga. Whenever things seemed to be improving the simplest action would suddenly cause a pain flare up. I tore the beads off despondently and cried. It wasn't even a heavy necklace. Snivelling, I passed the necklace across to Eric who duly inspected it and thought I should show it to my GP (not for repair you understand but for him to feel the weight of it). Well, I did just that at my next visit to Dr B. But he obviously misunderstood the point of the exercise at first. As I placed the necklace in his hand Dr B looked at it, smiled, said it was very pretty and handed it back to me (I wonder about doctors sometimes). He wasn't very informative about my pain flare up either, but said not to worry, I could use the necklace as weight guide to see how my neck was improving over time. What did he mean? Weeks? Months? Anyone's guess? I gave up and told him that I was fed up and tired of lying around listening to my 'teach yourself' German language course and had trouble looking up the verbs. This wasn't just because most of them were missing from the book but mainly because it hurt my neck to read it. This puzzled Dr B a bit. I don't know whether he'd found the same problem with a German course but or not. He scratched his head and said he really didn't know what to suggest.

Before I left, dear old Dr B suggested some antibiotics for the cough I had been trying to stave off for two weeks as he didn't want to risk it developing and shaking all my chest muscles about again. Although, I suspect it was just a precaution to save him having to see me anytime soon for a prescription.

With my prescription in hand I wandered off from the surgery, planning to check those antibiotics out with my personal pharmacist, Mr Gobi, before any intake of medication. Mr G and I had struck up quite a useful relationship over the past few months. He'd been the first person to advise me about leaving my surgical collar off as it would waste my neck muscles. I'd informed Dr B about this when he too suggested I leave it off. Looking back, I may have been a bit tactless on that particular visit as I remember, every time he explained anything about my 'condition' I found myself repeating more than once, 'That's what the pharmacist told me.'

I am pretty sure I saw Dr B grit his teeth as he asked: 'Who *is* this pharmacist?' I explained how helpful Mr G had been and about his kind offer to accompany me to the pain clinic in two months' time to help me to ask 'the right' questions.

We appeared to have a lot in common Mr Gobi and I, as we share a suspicion of doctors. Surprisingly, Dr B agrees with us on this one which, I think, is very broadminded of him. The pharmacist, on the other hand, may have harboured a bit of professional jealousy. Anyway, they have both confused me now as the pair of them told me to start putting the collar back on again! Do either of them know what they are up to?

I'll tell you something about Doctors, they love working in percentages but fall down badly on timescale calculations. They can say things such as: 'You have a sixty to seventy per cent chance of getting better,' and give no indication of how long it may take or what 'getting better' means. I might as well ask them 'how long is a piece of string'. One time when I asked for a fuller explanation of what I had done to myself when the blind hit me I was told that 'looking back is negative', that I should 'look to the future instead'. It was hard to get a grip on what that future might be with no timespan to work from. This was a person who was used to looking after two diaries and a wall chart. It strikes me that patients have to do more managing of doctors than the other way around. I don't find doctors' vague philosophical answers very helpful. Their responses usually throw me off the track for a while until I arrive home and realise that I have been hoodwinked again with no concrete opinion having been given. I wonder what a career service client would think if asked a question such as 'how do you become an accountant' and received the reply, 'with great difficulty'. In my role, at work, I could be severely reprimanded for this. Doctors earn a fortune and many of them were trained at the expense of sick tax payers like myself and it seems they can say what they like. There is little justice for patients due to the professional prestige and power that doctors can wield. Patients who display any over curiosity about a complaint can be labelled as unduly stressed and anxious just for wanting to find out what is going on with their own bodies. I think people in glass houses shouldn't throw stones because some statistics show that doctors have very high stress levels, alcoholic tendencies and one of the highest rates of suicide. Let them argue with that!

I am feeling very argumentative today on account of being fat and writing it all out is very therapeutic. Maybe that's another idea for a book? I could start off with a few notes for a patients' leaflet…

Tips on how to manage your doctor

The first thing to bear in mind is that doctors generally a have little in the way of communication skills. They are not to blame for this of course because their brains are jam packed with important scientific information. This means that the basic interaction skills required for one-to-one communication is not high on their list of priorities.

If the NHS realised how much money could be saved by making doctors more 'user friendly' I'm sure they would do something more about it pretty quickly. Thankfully, medical schools have picked up on this and some welcome arts and humanities qualifications along with the required sciences in the hope of attracting people who have something other than scientific interest and the will to become a doctor. However, what of those who have been in the profession for some time? After years of carrying the heavy burden of responsibility for making life and death decisions by necessity, many build themselves up in their heads to be gods. [1]

Whatever communication skills training is undertaken there is always the possibility that it will be open to classical psychological interpretation. Therefore, in order to set up any valuable two way conversation it is advisable for patients to avail themselves of some background information on the theories of Freud, Yeung and a few of the more recent psychological theorists. Patients will require this information in order to see themselves through the eyes of the doctor. In other words, 'If Mohammed won't go to the mountain, the mountain must go to Mohammed'. Get it?

A few 'don'ts' to remember for the consulting room

---

[1] Footnote: (Even he is meant to listen and to understand people).

1) Don't ask too many direct questions. This is their department. Direct questions from the patient may be interpreted as: a) anxiety or b) competitiveness.

2) Don't say 'I don't understand' too many times. They may think you haven't listened so won't tell you so much next time. They won't remember that you haven't spent five or six years at medical school, nor had their 'on the job' experience. They will think only that you haven't got their brains (which in my case is probably true). Doctors prefer to tell you only once about things. If you don't take it in the first time, write them a letter. It will save you both a lot of time and irritation.

3) Don't show any unnatural curiosity or hesitation about their suggested treatment. It makes them twitch.

4) Don't attempt to make any diagnosis about yourself that they haven't made first (they could put you down as neurotic. Remember, they have so much power you could end up in a strait jacket).

5) When a doctor uses that popular psychological tool 'the silence treatment' you must be quick enough to spot it and keep your mouth shut. You might be considered unnaturally talkative, unable to stand quiet interludes and be suffering from some deep mental agitation.

6) If you don't talk at all you could be diagnosed as mute but this could be preferable to the diagnosis cited in 5.

The end

Chapter 12

Lunch at Ciao Bellini

Today I was promised the dubious treat of lunch with my mother. We took a cab to a restaurant in Blackheath Village where I propped Mum and her stick up against an estate agent's wall while I nipped to a shop across the road to buy some cigarettes. On trying to return, I had great difficulty getting back across the road due to traffic build up. Not having on my surgical collar to indicate that I probably couldn't move very fast, I waited nervously for a gap in the traffic. After several minutes a car stopped to let me pass. As I turned to give a grateful signal to the driver a very nice looking young man returned me a beaming smile and seemed to be staring at my legs. I had put on so much weight around the hips that my skirt had risen up about four inches more than I normally wore it. Strange creatures, men, they didn't care whether there were fat fifty-year-old legs that were on show or not, just as long as they could see them. This was definitely a 'leg' man. Grateful that the skirt had proved such a useful replacement to the surgical collar, I retrieved mother from against the wall and led her into Ciao Bellini to eat. We were shown to a table at ground floor level in order to accommodate Mum's walking difficulty. We sat ourselves down at table to find the sun shining through the open door on a blissfully bright afternoon. However, within minutes, Mum began to shiver. Oh no! It had been the wrong choice on my part again. Trying to stay cheerful for my benefit, Mum weighed up the options of whether to stay put? Or move further inside the restaurant? No, she decided, we were fine and she would to stay put. In spite of this decision, M shot a grimace at the door every few seconds to show her discomfort. I could feel the muscles in my neck contracting uneasily as I wondered whether we were nonetheless, to go through the performance of changing tables or ask the waitress to close the door. A young, smiling Italian girl came over and took our order before I could give it further thought. We ordered fish for me and escalope Milanese for Mum. Only the escalope was to be served without the Milanese sauce and minus its normal accompaniment listed on the menu: pasta. By the time the order arrived accompanied by a dish of table d'hôtel vegetables the escalope Milanese bore little resemblance to its original description. Despite this, mother seemed happy and in between bending my aching neck to retrieve her stick which kept falling to the floor, I felt relatively relaxed and ordered wine for us both, with the intention of keeping her conversation light-hearted and my mind able to switch it all off. The waitress put in an appearance again brandishing what looked like a long metal pipe from which she offered us a seasoning of black pepper. 'Oh no,' said Mum, 'I can't take condiments.' M went on to elucidate this point by explaining that this was due to her high blood pressure and heart trouble. I said a secret prayer to myself that she wouldn't go on to explain about her angina, anaemia and the 'bad toe' that was stepped on by a soldier in a dance hall during World War Two. Fortunately, Mum started eating instead. Her usual complaint of 'too much food on the plate' wasn't made and the escalope disappeared from sight within minutes. I was soon to discover that most of it had been discretely wrapped up in her homemade doggie bag (table napkin) destined for the stomach of the cat at home. I tried not to let this irritate me as it usually did, drank my wine and tried to relax. Mum relaxed too and began to sip at her wine having calculated it was safe to drink because six hours had elapsed since her last intake of blood pressure medication. We chatted for a bit with Mum talking in an unusually high voice about her last electricity bill which too, seemed to have been rather high. I suggested Mum lower her voice as she proceeded to give a full explanation of how much money she normally 'put by' for this and that bill. The restaurant was becoming quite full and I didn't think diners would appreciate being given a run-down of her accounts. Mum never took kindly to her fifty-year-old daughter telling her what to do, so gave me a soothing smile and told me not to be silly. Even this announcement was made in too loud a voice so I ordered the bill and we left soon after. Though not before polishing off a cassata each (none of which ended up in the doggy bag owing to mother's sweet tooth) and coffees (although Mum's had to be practically minus the beans of course, to reduce her intake of caffeine).

Once outside Ciao Bellini, we crossed the road for a quick browse in the Oxfam shop. I bought an expensive (£5) good quality blouse and Mum, another very nice two-toned one, which we both knew she would never put on in case someone had died in it. I knew the wine was doing its job when I was able to observe her become more jovial, hearty and in benevolent spirits. I went over to the till to pay a sweet, rather doddery little lady assistant for our purchases. As I handed over the cash, Mum asked the assistant to provide us with two separate receipts but as she did so, made a mistake over the prices and confused the proceedings. I felt sorry for our sales assistant. She seemed like someone trying to rehabilitate herself after a nervous breakdown with Mum on the way to give her another. Fortunately, owing to Mum's kind and sympathetic nature she had quickly come to the same conclusion about the assistant's vulnerability as I had. With this in mind, M shot the woman a very sweet smile and complimented the assistant on the range of goods on display. We left the shop with Mum smiling, waving goodbye and promising to return the following week for some napkin rings.

When we did return a week later for those wonderful table adornments we were served by a new assistant. I am not sure what happened to the other one but I do hope it was nothing to do with our previous afternoon visit to her place of work!

Chapter 13

Stateside

A letter arrived today from my friend Gill who lives near Chicago. Gill wanted me to get hold of some embroidery wool for an elderly friend and forwarded a rather sweet letter from the lady. For authenticity, it reads much better with an American accent if you can manage that it in your thoughts. I must say though, I do not understand what 'world politics' prevents her buying her 'yarn' in the USA?

Dear Gillian,

I had one itty bitty of yarn on top of the incomplete project. I hope it is enough to match something like off white or oyster white. Bucilla No. 101 – I think. The paper wrap has disappeared. Whatever, if, as we say, no dice. Then I'll pick out the large areas and devise a border of a different colour.

After all the little yak, I decided to bake cookies and managed fairly well with sitting down only once to stir the heavy dough. You will get a sample next week. I also decided it was foolish of me to keep stitcheries here that few people realise what and why so, I am sending you the bargello piece. It is framed but if the frame isn't suitable, you can make a pillow top from it. I remembered what happened when Grandma left us. There were a few vultures who took a few things that were dear to others in the family. And, the stories my Jewish friend told me when her sisters died made my hair curl. I hope you will like it. I had fun doing it but went back to needlepoint.

The sun decided to stay out but a few renegade raindrops fell on Brownie who came in muddy as usual. The pink dogwood is in full bloom and the rhododendrons in front are beginning to show colour but the blooms are not as large as they were last year; late spring and too much rain.

Take care and thanks heaps for looking for the yarn. I never dreamed world politics would affect the state of yarn!

Love always,
Pam
(and a woof from Brownie).

So I went in search of the aforesaid 'yarn' as explained in my next letter to Gill:

Dear Gill,

At long last I've managed to remember to take your friend's wool to John Lewis and match it up. What a task that proved to be, especially for someone like me who is colour-blind. Anyway, I didn't do as badly as I'd imagined although though the sales assistant who helped me was faster at finding the right matches. We took four skeins out into the street because I said that the lighting inside the store was rubbish and I was right too. We were both a bit scared doing this in case the shop alarm went off. I said that although I might be the one to be arrested at least I couldn't be given the sack. The assistant said she'd find it a bit of a relief to be sacked. That just shows you the state that the British workforce is in!

I hope your friend finds that one of the enclosed colours fits in with her embroidery piece as we couldn't find a perfect match, though one looks passable. I think it is 465 though I've noticed the number has worn off a bit due to me being caught in the rain. What an idiot I am, but you already know that.

Yes, I am still at home, not working and it is all a long story so if you find time to give me a ring I will fill you in things a bit if you can stand it. Basically, I have gone from pillar to post trying out different treatments, all to end up at square one. Today I had to complete an action plan for the pain clinic on how to get myself fit! If I knew that would I be going to the hospital? The whole world seems to be off its head sometimes or is it me? Don't answer that truthfully (if you value our friendship). Everything else at home is OK but I could do with a good dose of one of our days out together and a good heart to heart chat. I am so lucky with my friends. Thank God they are all as 'off the wall' as I am so don't seem to notice that I'm nuts.

Suffice it to say I've worn out poor old GP Dr B, and that takes some doing as he has eleven kids to cope with. I fear that Dr De Souza, the consultant at the pain clinic, had her suspicions about my sanity yesterday when I described the symptoms I had developed as a result of her acupuncture. Dr De Souza said she had never heard anything like it in all her years administering acupuncture. She'd had strong reactors who had fainted and vomited, with symptoms coming on immediately or, within forty-eight hours. She had never, ever, had a patient develop stomach ache and headache that lasted for more than two weeks after treatment or not be able to sleep because of pains in their feet! If you know anyone in the USA who is an expert on strong reactors to acupuncture please see what you can find out for me. I am scared to ask anyone anything these days as I am sure they think I make it all up.

I hope Bob and the boys are well and happy and of course, you too. Still running around the block and having the odd sherry with Eleanor on the way back? – I hope so.

Tell your friend to let me know ASAP about the yarn and I will happily get more if one or other of them is of any use. They worked out at fifty-nine pence each so it is not a problem. Just let me know which ones to buy.

Love to you all,
B x

Chapter 14

A Second Retreat

My friend May P had been having a hard time with her mother Doris, of late. That dear lady could be difficult to deal with and sometimes there was just no pleasing her. May was exhausted having to sort out D's social service support, visit her daily and at the same time entertain three Spanish visitors at her own home. Knowing I was about to go for another stint of acupuncture that would probably leave me feeling wrecked I suggested we go to the East Delling Retreat Centre together for a couple of days. May isn't of any religious persuasion but she does so much voluntary work that in my eyes she is a modern-day saint in the truest sense. She is mainly an atheist and on her more vulnerable days, an agnostic. In spite of her doubts about 'organised' religion, May willingly accepted my invitation to try out the retreat centre as a night's alternative to B & B. So, we set off to East Delling driven by her spouse dear old Sidney. As with my husband Eric, three months earlier, Sidney was in no hurry to hang around the centre and May and I were soon deposited into our separate rooms overlooking a field of grazing horses. I took to the atmosphere again like a duck to water and was immediately transported into a world of peace, spirituality and trust. May, on the other hand, was not experiencing the same spiritual relief. She was locked in her bedroom holding the door handle which had come off in her hand. After fiddling around with the lock for some time, May managed to position the handle on to its spindle and get the door to open, at which point we both went off to look for help. We found Sr Benedict in her office from whom we requested a screwdriver to fix the handle back on again. The three of us returned to May's room with the screwdriver and secured the handle to the door. Wisely in my opinion, May decided to hang on to the screwdriver in case the door should jam again with her inside unable to escape the room. When Sr Benedict was out of earshot my M confided that it would also serve as a weapon should the need arise. I wasn't quite sure what my friend had in mind until she confided that she'd noticed a shortish, strange, suspicious looking man wearing pebbled glasses. I could see the 'simple trust' part of the retreat experience hadn't quite rubbed off on May when she also said she was also very anxious to meet the secretary and pay off her B & B before anyone stole her money.

Taking advantage of the peace and silence of the building, we led off into our respective rooms for an afternoon nap. I was awakened an hour later by my friend who poked her head around the door to say she was going for a walk. I elected to rest a bit longer so away went my friend for her walk after ticking me off for leaving my door unlocked while there was a man in pebbled glasses at large. I wondered whether people in pebbled glasses ought to be covered by the Equal Opportunities Discrimination act? May voicing her views so loudly in such a place of peace seemed even worse as we were all meant to be one big family. Nothing I could do about that I decided so, I drifted off for a few more minutes before May returned suggesting we visit the chapel that she had noticed a signpost for. Thinking this a good idea we set off together to find its whereabouts. Locating it being not as simple as we had imagined, we found ourselves opening various doors leading on to seminar rooms, kitchens and rest places. The chapel when we did find it, was seemingly empty until we noticed a flicker of black, a darting figure moving quickly between two side entrances. At first we thought it a religious apparition and I swear I witnessed May's hair stand on end for a few seconds. We both breathed a sigh of relief when the figure appeared again at the main door carrying a box of candles and we recognised it as that of Sr Anne. Alone once more in the chapel I heard May call out, 'Sister Anne, Sister Anne is there anybody there?' Apparently this was a quotation from a film of *Peter Pan*. I had never heard this one before but we both began to giggle like schoolgirls playing a prank. We muttered a quick prayer in case we had upset any one from the spiritual world before taking off for a walk in the rose garden where I introduced May to the delights of tree hugging. She was hesitant at first and placed a loose, clearly embarrassed arm around a weedy little tree (in a thicket in case she was overlooked by another visitor). I boldly displayed my ability for big hugs to a wonderful leafy oak tree I was familiar with from my last visit. I did have to put my dark blue jacket on back to front though, to avoid getting my tee shirt dirty. I loaned it to May afterwards who had another go at hugging and tried the big oak tree herself while I had a cuddle with a silver birch. With May now wearing her own jacket back to front we were really getting to grips with our 'one- ness' with the earth and journeyed daintily from tree to tree enjoying our communion with nature. Such serenity was soon dissipated when we became aware of an elderly couple seated on a bench staring at us (one of whom was wearing pebbled glasses). *Hmm*, I thought, *now who thinks who is suspicious?* In any event, we decided it was time to make a discreet exit from the garden and return to the centre in time for afternoon tea.

The following day, we contemplated a walk to the village of East Delling. It was a beautiful sunny Sunday just right for a peaceful walk along a quiet country road with only the singing of birds for company. Nothing passed us along the road with the exception of a car or two at intervals. We made our way in the direction of a large green field that seemed just right for a short break, meditation and a bit of tree hugging if there was one available. To reach the field, we had to turn left into a mud track that ran between two large houses, but as we did so, all hell seemed to break loose. We were greeted at the gate by two furious looking bulldogs and a frisky horse peering over a hedge to the right of us. I instinctively turned to run but quickly realised what a pointless endeavour it would be. I was unable to out run anyone in my current condition and certainly not two dogs. Being a real animal lover, May managed to hide any fear she might have from the dogs by addressing them rather chummily. This may have made her feel better but I'm not sure the dogs felt the same way for they continued to bark as I tip-toed around the other side of the house to hide myself. Backing away to the rear wall, I felt someone behind me and walked straight in to a pair of green wellied feet that were attached to a very tall, aristocratic looking lady with blond hair. 'Lady' took control of the situation immediately. The dogs stopped yapping, the horse shut up and May bid her a jolly good morning and got back on to the road where I hastily joined her. Continuing along the road we discovered a bridleway that looked as though it gave access to 'our' field and as we walked along it, it became more and more muddy around the foot area but happily, we experienced no other problems. We did eventually reach our green field which lived up to expectations being beautifully verdurous, butter cupped in places and surrounded by ancient oaks. Heaven, we thought, and sat down on the grass to take in the view across the downs. We even had a makeshift picnic with two marathon bars and a couple of small cartons of orange juice I had brought from home. There were a few cows in the distance, munching contentedly on the new grass. I think we must have dozed off for no more than a few minutes when I became aware of a gentle thudding noise bringing me to my senses. Sitting bolt upright I perceived a cow, or maybe bull that seemed to be in a bit of a hurry to reach our side of the field. I nudged May awake and we were on our feet quite rapidly, this time trying to exit the field faster than the animal heading our way. *More haste less speed* was written for me because the faster I tried to move the more difficult things became. First, I trod in a cow pack then fell into the mud as soon as we reached the bridleway. In spite of being nearly ten years my senior, May managed to get to the retreat centre in one piece with just a bit of mud on her shoes while I smelled like a dairy farm and with mud all up my legs. Having missed out on lunch through knapping though, I am just grateful those pursuant beasts granted us enough time to digest the marathon bars earlier!

On our arrival we walked passed Sister Anne, who tactfully averted her eyes as on our approach and 'Pebble Glasses' too, whose eyes seemed even more magnified as he came near. We retired to our respective rooms in silence where I for one, fell asleep until supper time.

Chapter 15

A Date with Dracula?

I had made a promise to myself that the next time I met Dr Ling I'd be a bit more tactful having received the impression at the last visit that he found me a bit 'over the top'. This was apparent on one particular occasion when I had raised my voice with frustration on wanting an explanation as to all the fuzzy bits on my X-ray. Buddhists clearly have a dislike of raised voices. Another time there was the incident when I was peeved at not getting an answer about the pain I had when trying on my birthday present (the handmade necklace). So, at the next appointment I would make clear that I had worked the necklace business out for myself without his help by suggesting that it had been transferred pain coming from the 'iffy' discs. Yes, he had agreed, this was probably the case. He still dodged the question about the fuzziness and my C7 disc though. This calmness and refusal to be drawn about any opinion was not helpful and made me feel worse about things. I really wanted to understand what had happened to my neck and shoulders. When Dr Ling said that I should learn to do things in stages, he received a sharp response from me when I said testily that I couldn't do anything in stages. Instead of snapping back, which I thought he might, Dr L invited me to follow him into the treatment room where I sat down and jabbered away saying that I knew he often delivered acupuncture just to shut me up as I couldn't remember anything after the needles went in. 'Yes, that's right,' came the sotto voiced confirmation as Dr L jabbed away with the pins and I drifted once more into no man's land and all stress disappeared.

As much as I joked about acupuncture there was certainly something required to help me cope with the endless wait for the upper regions to recover properly. My mind often went into overdrive because it had nothing useful to focus on. I couldn't stand the vagueness of everything and not being able to tell 'work' when and how I might be able to return to my job. I constantly asked myself what was going on with my body. Why was I able to do certain things one day but not the next? I needed answers just to be able to manage the misery of being this 'other' person who couldn't do anything of any consequence i.e. work, write much, even play with my granddaughters without risking a flare up in condition. At least my strong reaction to acupuncture suggested there could be benefits long as well as short term, albeit slow progress.

The next time I visited Dr L it had to be at his practice in Sussex on account of the London clinic being fully booked. The journey involved catching first, a train and then a taxi. Under Dr L's command I could then find my own way back to the station on foot after treatment as it was, according to him, 'rather a pleasant walk'. I thought about this plan for a moment and wondered why I might need a taxi to get there but could be relied upon not to get lost on the way back when I would probably be feeling as high as a kite after the treatment? A thought passed through my mind that it might be the fact that I would be walking back to the station minus his cheque payment rather than to him with it. Charitably, I dismissed this suspicion and decided that Dr L simply did not want me to be late and mess up his appointments, hence the taxi ride and probably recommended the walk back because it would be good for my health.

So, arriving at my destination in the said taxi, I was deposited in a quiet little road that went up a hill. On Dr Ling's front door there was type written note pinned to it with instructions to 'knock first and enter'. Half imagining that this message held eerie undertones, I wondered if I might I might be entering a place akin to Dracula's castle. Knocking and pushing open the door as instructed, I was led into a perfectly ordinary hallway and greeted by a strange sound which seemed to emanate from the staircase. This proved to be the croaky voice of Dracula, aka Dr Ling with a sniffy cold and minus the fangs. In his usual bossy tone, Dr L directed me to the waiting room where I sat down and gazed through the French doors overlooking the garden. I couldn't help thinking how practical and beautifully ignored it all looked. Every bit of it was paved with the exception of a small patch where a poplar tree swayed defiantly in the wind. I loved looking at grass and flowers but if ever required to tend a garden myself I've always said it would have to be resurfaced like a car park tout de suite! No marked bays of course, but most of the earth cemented over with a few odd flower pots dotted around close to each other so I would not have to walk too far to water them. We had a lovely garden at home but Eric took care of ninety-five per cent of it. My efforts were confined to giving a yearly snip to the roses and forsythia at the front of the house plus look after the area under the big apple tree, the 'fairy dell' as I called it. In truth, I hadn't done any of this for years and any resident fairies would have been strangled to death by the long vine weed that had taken over. Because of my neglect, Eric had removed this responsibility from me along with his permission to give the forsythia a quick back and sides in the autumn. I suspect he couldn't wait to do this as he was without any understanding as to why I liked to get it a bit like one of Van Gogh's trees being a Constable man himself. As with most things, we had directly opposed tastes. That's why our house was what you might call 'theme-less'. It didn't seem to stop people filling it up though and making themselves at home. They all seemed to like the house as it was. Not so my eldest son and that may have been one of the reasons he ended up in China. Peter liked precision and order and could never understand why we didn't have anything in the house that matched up. Once when he was giving me one of his interior design lectures I reminded him just who actually owned the house. It was our business how we chose to decorate and when he had a place of his own he could do what he liked with it. Now that he is living in Hong Kong, I haven't yet seen the mistakes made in his own accommodation, but judging by the monstrosity of a bed he bought for his room in our house, I bet there are a few.

My imaginings and reflections were shortly interrupted by the catarrhal voice of Dracula summoning me to 'cumb upstairs' for treatment. Dr L apologised for having the cold and asked me how I had been before reading up on his notes of when and where he'd punctured last time. I could sense that talking was even more difficult for him with his cough and cold so took over and began to advise him about what remedies to try for his cold before my suggestions were brought to a halt by the needles (what a perfectly, good, legal way to get your own back I thought). That was before I was stopped from thinking of course, due to the acupuncture. The phone in the next room rang twice while I was sat on the treatment table. Apparently, the call was from a lost patient trying to find the surgery. After the second call, Dr Ling returned with a smile on his face saying that he thought the caller, a new patient, was 'a bit scatty'. I smiled too, though I wasn't sure he should have made that comment one patient to another. It did make me feel hopeful though that perhaps he hadn't spotted quite how dippy his present patient was.

Feeling relaxed, heady and free of pain, I thanked Dr L and started to climb down from the couch, but as I did so, he leapt up shouting, 'No, no, the needles are still in.' I really had no idea they were still there as I had been unable to feel or think a thing. I sat down to have them removed and just about managed the concentration to write out a cheque and make an appointment for next time.

I was led slowly to the front door armed with a small map drawn on an old envelope by Dr Ling where I was to find my way to the station by way of the 'pleasant walk' to town. This I managed to do, as well as catch the right train, fall asleep on it and as a result, end up at London Bridge Station. This was actually about seven miles away from where I wanted to be. I did get home eventually and also managed the recommended hot shower before collapsing onto the bed in a pleasant state of stupefaction.

All in all, it was not a bad day.

Chapter 16

Goodbye Boots and All That

My health visits to Sussex instead of London became habitual. I never really minded these on account of the scenic views from the train and the sight of Dr L's bare garden again, which I always found strangely serene. What added to its appeal was the fact that it seemed to require little or no work. The last time I had seen it there was not a plant or flower to be seen, just a solitary evergreen tree on a sunless winter's day. The peace of it was often in my thoughts and I would reflect on the damp unkempt slabs of the pathway owned by someone obviously uncaring of daily chores. I wasn't even sure who, exactly, lived in the house and it had the feel of a property mainly kept empty. I knew that Dr L worked at his London clinic Tuesday to Thursday and that he always saw his 'Sussex patients' on a Friday. At morning appointments Dr L's hair always looked wet. I imagined he dashed home on Thursday evenings, crashed out after a stressful few days in London and had a bit of a lie in on Friday, and then a quick shower before the first patient. For a man who hardly spoke, he could be quite amusing when he chose to be so. I often had a chuckle to myself too, about the way he combed his wet hair down flat as a pancake in an effort to obliterate any wave or curl. He also sported different shoes on a Friday. Not the London type (Oxford Brogues) but black slip on shoes with a little toggle on the front, the style I recollect being popular in the eighties.

Today was to be a visit where he would take stock of my medical progress in order to write up a full report on injuries.

Dr L spent a while in an apparently serious and quizzical mood gazing at his folder with raised eyebrows while I gazed down at his Friday shoes. 'I seem to have made rather a lot of notes last time,' he said.

Thinking to amuse him I replied, 'Wait until you get the others from my GP... there'll be half a century's worth.'

I was a bit disappointed at his reply: 'I'll bet,' he murmured. What a cheek! You would think that at fifty quid a throw he could manage something better such as, *and I expect they will make very interesting reading too.* Never mind, after a year of me he couldn't really be expected to keep his true thoughts hidden all the time. Even Dr B was running out of jobs for me to do and medical breakthroughs to inform him about just to keep me occupied. Dr B had moved on from elevating me from a 'would be' designer of medical aids to the suggestion of spending two hours a week helping out in a hospital. The comparison seemed to me like demotion from doctor to sluice cleaner (though probably closer to my ability at the moment). While I appreciated this job idea, I probably spent more time at hospital than at home these days anyway.

Dr Ling asked how I felt. I told him about my current backache and suggested that it might be my own fault and due to the heels on my new boots. 'Oh yes,' he said. 'They are a bit high and very stiff too,' glaring down at them at their place of abandonment in the corner of the room. Somehow, in these new clinical surroundings my little black leather boots no longer appeared stylish and Parisian but just plain flashy. Even the buckles seemed to be trying to conceal themselves behind the chair legs. The wrinkled leather at the ankles reminded me of Jane Avril in Toulouse Lautrec's posters and completely out of place in a surgery in a little Sussex village; the boots of a woman of dubious character.

While Dr L returned to reading his notes, I thought I'd give him a quick update of my right arm. 'I don't suppose you are interested,' I started, 'but now my neck is feeling better and my arm without that blocked feeling I can tell that I am cramping it up when I write. The hospital had advised me to practise making circular movements but that seemed suspiciously like polishing to me so I wondered whether I might try my hand at oil painting instead.'

Without looking up from his clipboard he said, 'Just keep it down when you are writing OK?' After a minute or two Dr L (alias Dracula sans fangs) stopped reading and gave me some acupuncture before asking me whether I would like my neck 'tugged'.

'What do you think?' I said.

'Well, it's up to you,' he replied.

Not used to this level of responsibility about my own treatment I decided to leave well alone. 'I think we'll leave it this week,' I told him importantly, already thinking of the 'pleasant' walk I would take on the way back to the station.

Ten minutes later, whilst tottering along the road in my boots came the realisation that I had left my map to the station at home so would have to try and remember the way to it after last time. Well, what do you know? The pretty tree-lined street eventually led me straight to a view of Homebase, smacking of suburbia and important boring tasks such as food shopping. However, just opposite I spotted the old railway station. Being a steam train enthusiast I was keen to take a peek at one but sadly was out of luck. A large notice on the gate read: 'Closed for Engineering works'. *Quel dommage!* I thought, as Jane Avril might have said, *What a pity!* I hung over the gate for a while in an acupunctured haze and wandered about a bit feeling slightly lost and not caring (my usual state after treatment). *Oh well*, I thought, *Ce la vie' isn't it?* And plodded on once more to find the railway station for home.

Chapter 17

Mother at the Hospital

Obviously not realising what a leading question it was, the nurse called out, 'So how are you feeling?' I opened my mouth to give her a short summary of the current, family, worries I had; Uncle Sid and his disorientating memory loss, my mother's depression, Eric's diabetes, and my knee (the neck trouble spoke for itself as it was back in the brace again). I closed my mouth again quickly after realising that the nurse had been really addressing my mother. She wasn't to be disappointed by a lack of response. Once in the consulting room Mum poured forth her usual admirably factual but confusing, medical history designed to test the listening skills of even the most experienced medic. During frequent visits to various medical establishments with my mother I have observed that young doctors give her the greatest sympathy. They admire her wit and adroitness and marvel at her age. They must see it as a challenge when she fires a volley of symptoms at them with a few random dates thrown in to confuse the issue. The older doctors know better. They've seen it all before and know that all she really needs is a prescription for anything, because whatever they give her won't work but will at least prove that they have taken her seriously. What really fool them all are the answers she gives to seemingly simple questions such as: 'How are you feeling right now?' (I gather what they want to hear is 'this or that hurts' plus where and how often.) Instead, her 'normal informative response' takes one of three forms:

1. I have never felt as bad as this in my life.
2. I just feel ill.
3. I'm not at all well.

Try as they might try to make her, there is no way M is going to reveal to them what or where her symptoms might be coming from. The only clue that she will give them is to tell whether she is better, worse, or about the same as she was yesterday. Ho hum.

Mum and I sat ourselves down in suite four and waited to be summoned by the nurse. M was weighed, questioned and deposited back in her seat for a further five minutes before going to meet the consultant. Once called in to the room, M disappeared behind a screen with a nurse and the doctor who asked her: 'Would you say you were a person who prefers to feel too hot or too cold?'

I couldn't resist answering for her: 'Neither. It is either too hot or too cold.'

I heard the nurse giggle and say, 'Your daughter says there is no pleasing you.' *Too right*, I thought, though said nothing. Mum emerged from the screen chattering away to the doctor, wanting to know the reason for this, that, why and how, concerning the state of her health. When the consultant posed some questions to Mum, I tried to intervene and tell him some things I knew to be true. I did this to save us all from the confusion of Mum's answers (she was good at questions but not so hot on expressing her answers concisely).

'Do you mind?' she said to me, indignantly. 'I can speak for myself!'

And so she continued to do so then, as always and evermore.

Amanda,

I am writing this very early in the morning because my time clock is all wrong. It's 3.40am and I have had cornflakes and whiskey in hot water because of my cold.

Did I tell you about the time I was nearly pregnant at forty-nine? Well, I had to go to the doctor of course and didn't know whether it was the big P or the big M creeping up on. I had left things one week which I thought was sensible; didn't want to panic myself. I told the doctor about my fears and rather thought as it had been only one week since the 'crime' he might be able to give me a pill to sort things out. I was shocked to discover that I was three days too late for any preventative treatment but informed the doctor that I wouldn't dream of doing anything other than continue the pregnancy. I almost wish I hadn't said anything at all that day as he leapt to his feet, slapped me on the back and told me that I was a woman after his own heart (??!). He couldn't see any reason why an older woman couldn't have a perfectly healthy foetus and would arrange for me to have a proper pregnancy test. While he was in a receptive mood I thought I would take the opportunity to tell him about the pain in my knee and the pain in my right hip just above my past bikini line. I say 'past' because all my bikinis had been relegated to the 'just in case' drawer for beachwear. Just in case I should suddenly appear ten years younger and lose a stone in weight. The doctor immediately announced that this was probably arthritis which would probably leave me after I had given birth. His enthusiasm was amazing but I wasn't sure whether I would have anything to look forward to or not. On the one hand possible arthritis and a possible cure; on the other an unexpected arrival, along with no money and not even a cure for my new affliction. While he wrote up my notes I sat there trying to take it all in. There was a picture in my head of a little boy about seven years old playing rugby. His two grey-haired aged parents stood by at the edge of the pitch cheering him on. One of them displayed a bandaged knee and was suffering from a bad case of heavy wrinkles.

When I found out a week later that I was not, in fact 'in the club' so to speak, both Eric and I went into the doldrums. We had geared ourselves up to eighteen years of stress, expense, aggravation, sleepless nights and a few years of smelly nappies sweetened by fun, cuddles and happy gurgles. Again, not sure what to celebrate as my arthritic knee had probably lost its reprieve.

Well, I do feel better for that so I might manage some sleep now before the nine am news bulletin. Zzzzzzzzzzzzzzzzzzzzzzz

Hope you find yourself in a better state than I am
B x

Chapter 18

Travel Notes

One year later:
Feeling desperately in need of a holiday and some blue skies, Eric and I had planned to take off to Spain for a short break. Unfortunately, just as I was beginning to plan my wardrobe, Eric announced that we would have to cancel the trip owing to his heavy work schedule. I was furious and bitterly disappointed. There was one chink of hope for me though as I knew that Zadie, May and Sidney were staying in Switzerland and I wondered if they would mind me flying out to visit them and locate a B & B somewhere close by?. I called Zadie who chatted to the others about the idea. Before long I had cleared off to Switzerland and joined the party which included May's sister Denise.

I was soon on the telephone to a little Pension in Kandersteg found on the internet. I telephoned and speaking in French, asked if we could converse in English. 'Madam,' came the frosty reply. 'I speak French, German, English and Italian, what would you prefer?' I thanked her and requested that we stick to English, then asked if there were might be any en suite rooms available for a few nights. 'Madame,' she retorted sharply. 'This is a Pension, not a five-star hotel!' I could see we were not off to a good start but as the Pension seemed close to my friends' apartment I decided to take any room available.

On arrival, I soon discovered that the quaint little abode I had booked myself into (Hotel Welcommen), had a charm more akin to its name than the friendliness extended. The owner who I called 'Frau Edelweiss', was indeed a formidable lady who did not respond kindly to my request for a call at 7am the next morning. There was no phone in my room of course and I did not own a mobile then. Frau E said she couldn't possibly give me an alarm call owing to the fact that she 'had no butler'. As I was only one of two guests staying there I didn't think it would be that much of a problem for her to give a knock at my door. Imagine my surprise the next morning when she wrapped heavily on the door and, called me for breakfast. Not only did I feel victorious in being granted a wake up but I wondered if we may have actually struck up a more amicable relationship. This thought was soon dispelled though, on the way to the dining room when I came across Frau E in the corridor and apologised for any inconvenience I may have caused her. Frau explained frostily that she had only given me a call me because she had to get up and let the cat out for 'a pee'. Not knowing how to respond to this piece of information, I scraped and bowed my way to the table for my anticipated crusty rolls and delicious coffee.

Breakfast was all I had imagined with the addition of a plastic alarm clock presented to me by Frau E to ensure I would never require a call from her, the butler, or anyone else in subsequent mornings. After breakfast I set off to meet Zadie and co for a walk up the little mountain (big hill) visible from my bedroom. It was turning out to be a rather lovely day with beautiful views to be spotted from every corner of the little town with brightly coloured flowers packing every window box in site. Our jolly little group assembled a few yards from my Swiss abode and off we went 'a wanderin' so to speak with our knapsacks on our backs (well one of us carried a plastic carrier bag truth to tell and Sidney you know who I refer to here), but there is ALWAYS SOMETHING isn't there? There had to be something capable of spoiling our ability to have fun as 'real hikers'. Zadie, in spite of her smiles was quieter than usual. Apparently, Denise had put Z on a diet in order for her to lose the two-stone postoperative weight she had put on. My dear friend was determined to get fit and lose the weight. Unfortunately, Z's appetite for food and sweets is equalled only by her sex drive, which by her reckoning is: 'A bit on the high side, dear.' You might think that one would cancel the other out and the sex use up some of the extra calories but not so in Z's case so maybe a lot of it is in her head. Judging by the way she flirts though, I know it is not out of her head for long. Zadie's sentences are often peppered with innuendoes and at the weakest excuse she will plonk a kiss on anyone's face, afterwards giving them marks out of ten for warmth. This is all harmless fun on her part for when Z is back home with her spouse they both act as though they are joined at the hip. I have never seen two people, so many years married, still arguing and still forgetting it the next minute and laughing as though they were twenty. Z reports to Rick by mobile several times a day from wherever in the world either of them happens to be. These reports take place in public toilets, on mountain tops wherever and whenever is felt necessary. Conversations are based on the most trivial subjects and domestic occurrences, which become over exaggerated in importance when they are apart from one another.

So, up the mountain road we hiked, May, Sidney and Denise in the lead with Zadie and me bringing up the rear puffing and chattering along the pathway picking flowers and wondering at the sights and sounds of nature all around us. Being so carried away with our surroundings that we hardly noticed the fact that we had lagged so far behind the others that they had disappeared from sight. We quickened our pace somewhat and after ten minutes arrived at a little makeshift café in the centre of a clearing where the others were partaking of some cool drinks. Being quite hot through hurrying Z and I sat down to join them with a nice cool drink of lemonade. We had hardly finished these when it was time to go. Denise instructed us firmly, to keep up with them all. This was imperative to do so too, as D was the only one to possessing a map. To be honest, even if we had one ourselves we probably wouldn't have been any better off .We certainly didn't want to get lost even though it was only a very small mountain and would have had no idea where we might be walking to and how to get back again. Setting off again we made great endeavours to be good hikers and with a struggle managed to stay with them. Zadie was doing particularly well considering the length of time since her op. I had my own back and shoulder problems and I could only carry a small bottle of water and a purse in my rucksack. As far as Z and I were concerned we were toughing it out in spite of adversity and gave each other a verbal pat on the back at every opportunity. Unbelievably, we all reached the summit together and looked down upon the most beautiful blue lake you can imagine. We sat down for an hour or two in the sun and met up with Jack, a friend of Denise who rather put Zadie and my exploits in the shade as he had pushed his mother all the way to the top in her wheelchair! He did look extremely fit and not surprisingly, so did mother. Neither of them seemed a bit phased about the return journey. I reflected on this while going back down the mountain; me carefully picking my way down the slopes and Zadie stretching out a hand to help me every so often!

Denise had informed us that there would be a little restaurant on a new route down the mountain's main path. It would be easy to find and it was situated to the right of the pathway, apparently. D was right about that position only Z and I reached it two hours after herself, May and Sidney. Just as we arrived and were about to order some food *they* set off to leave. I am convinced that we hadn't done anything to precipitate this exit just that none of them ever hangs about unnecessarily whereas Z and I seemed to be doing just that very thing all the time. Feeling as though we had failed yet again, my pal and I ordered wine and food and soon felt cheered. As I was tucking into the most exquisite chillied beef, I felt something scorch my throat and began a fit of coughing. My trusty friend Z leapt to her feet immediately and proceeded to belt the daylights out of my back to release whatever it might be from my throat while screaming out in English that her friend was choking and demanding someone bring water for me. I was very touched by this attention and while recovering, tried to tell her that there hadn't been anything stuck anywhere, but maybe the chilli aggravated my throat. It was just as well that I hadn't been choking as Z appeared to be the only other person interested. No one turned a hair even though the little place was packed with eaters. It was just like being at home in England. No one saw or heard a thing!

Later on our continued journey to the bottom of the mountain I told Zadie what a reliable friend she was and how touched I had been at her speedy response and obvious concern for me. Like two ten-year-olds we started picking wild flowers again with a view to drying them out and making pictures from them on reaching the UK. It was going to be my job to store them flat at the bottom of my suit case carefully wrapped in newspaper. That was the plan. Little did we know that it would be six or more months before I remembered them and even though the flowers were dead we *still* made our pictures. This determination must have been what carried us through a certain situation (and down the mountain at speed), when we suddenly recalled our promise to cook dinner for everyone in the group's apartment. It was also not a good sign when we discovered the time was almost 6pm and there was still the bottom of the mountain to reach. Our only hope was that we might find something equivalent to a late night mini market open and that was unlikely in a little village such as Kandersteg. The fear of being 'in trouble' again was enough to drive us on to devise a quick menu plan as we wended our way down. If all the shops were closed we would have to stand everyone a meal, if we were in luck and could find some chicken I would slice it and fry it in herbs and oil, while Zadie put together a rice salad. That dish, a bottle of wine and some cake might do the trick. Yes, we were in luck! The only shop we found open was a mini market due to close at 7pm and we had twenty minutes to spare. Managing to buy chicken, rice, sweetcorn, peas, green beans, herbs, chocolate cake, and a bottle of wine, we were up and off before you could say Frau Edelweiss. Unhappily, our arrival at the apartment was met by a very stony, book reading silence. Z and I said nothing and proceeded to start work in the kitchen as planned. We did well, my chum and me, and before too long we were all happily arranged around the table drinking and eating. *Cheers* we all said and *phew*, thought the two of us or in South London speak: WE DONE IT MAN!

Sadly, a day later I had to say goodbye to my friends as they took the train to D's flat in Basle and I was to spend two further nights alone in Kandersteg. This wasn't easy for a woman who had never lived alone but I made the best of it, enjoyed the sights, told myself it was good for my character and one evening alone in a restaurant decided to send a postcard to dear old Dr Ling. He was used to me complaining so thought he might appreciate finding out that I could also enjoy myself given the chance.

Dear Dr Ling,

As you are found of walking I thought you might be interested in this place. Having a lovely time and managed to climb a couple of small mountains yesterday (big ones for me) hence, I could now do with a couple of acupuncture stabs in my rucksack shoulder and since visiting Bern yesterday, an antibiotic jab in my left leg! Bern is a very pretty town but inhabited by some strange flying beetles which zoom up your trouser legs and sting you in the most inconvenient areas (well-illustrated by moi in the public war dance I did shortly after).

Wishing you a happy summer,
BW

Chapter 19

Oh Buddha and HMS Disaster!

Hi Amanda,

Gotta take a break from thinking about 'the book', which, after all this time, is nearly finished so planning to send you an oriental music cassette which is my latest stress buster (apart from drink and my drugs that is). Of course it may just give you a headache, but let me know if it works. Currently into creative visualisation, I have creatively visualised this (true) scene of events for you.

Let me take you to Lantau Island in Hong Kong. Imagine a hot day, a dusty road and a few wild dogs roaming about a dry tree lined patch of ground, looking shifty. Various local merchants are selling their wares (mainly, crisps and baked corn sticks) beneath the shadow of the biggest Buddha in the world (plus three other wise Buddhas, whose particular said wisdom I've forgotten). Anyway, it's a hot day, the Buddhas are out and so are the dogs. Eric and B are taking it in turns to snap at each other (verbally as well as with the camera), because there is little else to do in the heavy heat of the day. Only the Buddhas appear serene as they gaze imperiously out across the mountainside through the grey blue mist circling their shoulders. A few yards, distant, a Buddhist temple can be seen. The gentle sound of monks at prayer emanates from the yellow, gold and red temple.

Somewhere in a corner is Peter, taking a break from his parents and longing for them to get on with the tourist thing and wishing they could all make a break for the return ferry to the mainland. Unfortunately, Eric had drifted into one of his slow (I'm on holiday and relaxing) plods, walking in the sun with the protection of his panama hat. His wife was definitely into photographing everything in sight in case the monsoon was to come on anytime soon.

Eventually, the three of them came together at the foot of the temple steps and began their trek along the dusty road. As they did so they heard music coming from somewhere (a tourist stall selling CDs), which seemed to capture a little the tranquillity of the big Buddhas.

Yes, it really was like that. Comic at times, a few things went wrong that day because it was so hot, dry and slightly scary with the wild dogs BUT to see the Buddhas, to hear the monks chanting and listen to the beautiful language of Mandarin in song was unforgettable.

I put that music on whenever I feel stressed and all disharmony just melts away.

Good luck and let me know how things go.
B x

HMS Disaster: I had always wanted a remote controlled boat ever since my children's childhood. We never had the cash in those days to extend to such luxuries so made do with the little wooden variety. The type that cause no trouble, being devoid of complication other than requiring a long piece of string tied to the helm for retrieval purposes and a long cairn for tilting the boat upright on the occasion of a strong wind or low flying duck over the pond. This year I decided to 'push the boat out' for once (excuse the pun) and procure for myself such a maritime indulgence as a radio controlled battleship.

Its maiden voyage having gone pretty smoothly on Orpington pond, I invited my friends (May and Sidney) to accompany the grandchildren and me to try our luck on Blackheath pond. *Just like the old days*, I thought, as we settled down to watch seven-year-old Steven sail our impressive vessel on a smooth pond that was fast becoming deserted of the local birds and swans. As the sun streamed through the trees I munched a biscuit in the pleasant autumnal weather with little three-year-old Jemima sitting one side of me beside me and May on the other. We watched as Sidney walked off into the distance to seek out a free car park space. Sidney had already lost a one pound coin in the out of order parking machine closest to the pond so was not about to risk another and on the other hand did not wish to chance a fine.

Steven sailed the craft along the water its impressive little lights twinkling as it moved obediently along the water's edge. 'What about sailing it around the Island?' May called out to him. There was a large clump of bulrushes central to the pond.

'That's a good idea,' I agreed, not realising how tall the rushes were nor how easy it might be to get model ships caught up in them. Steven began to steer the boat around the island quite carefully and then guided it just a fraction closer to the edge of it. Close enough that is, for our battleship to experience its first altercation. There was no enemy sighted but the little ship could not seem to drag itself away from the island. Its lights twinkled and alarms bleeped as we all had a go at trying to drag the boat away from the reeds and rushes but the ship's Ariel was caught up and that was that. Nothing could move it. Twenty minutes later Sidney arrived back having managed to obtain free parking three quarters of a mile away. I felt sorry that S would not get his go at steering the ship now that it was stuck fast. Fortunately, Sidney had brought along a special boat hooker outer that he had fashioned from a bent wire coat hanger and a long cane. This was employed at speed as Sidney tried to hook the boat out from the reeds. Sadly, the island was so far away from the edge of the pond that he would only be able to reach it with the cane by floating out on a sun bed or sailing up to it on a dinghy; neither of which was at hand. It seemed the only way to retrieve our vessel was to wade out and untangle it by hand. I had no intention of doing this myself as I was scared of water. Whoever might attempt it would need waders on anyway. Fortunately, I knew just that person. He lived nine miles away but would oblige I was sure as his son had been the perpetrator of the accident. Suddenly, little Jemima began wriggling and squirming. These were both signs that we needed to find her a toilet double quick. I grabbed her hand and flew across the grass to a little café. No luck there for a toilet (or so they said), so I dashed next door to the pub. Hallelujah! We made it to the loo just in time. Next, I wandered down to the village with Jemima to locate a telephone box with the intention of making a call to the children's Dad, Peter. None of us had brought along a mobile phone! I did manage to find a call box but on picking up the receiver, found that it was not attached to anything! Walking back despondently to our boating chums, I was fortunate in finding another public pay phone which, again, I attempted to use. This time it ate up my last coins, but got me through to the number and allowed me to listen to the voice at the other end before going dead. By this time I was cold and tired, and so was Jemima. I half-carried half-walked her back to the others, who were still waiting by the pond with the sad marooned little battle ship. Sidney suggested we go home, leave the ship until the next day and return early in the morning with Peter and some waders. I wasn't keen on this suggestion saying that a captain never leaves his or her ship in peril and that I intended to contact Peter then sit and wait for him by the boat in case anyone decided to try and steal it.

Borrowing some coins from May, I returned to the previous phone box and this time established contact for a few seconds just managing to yell out that the boat was in the middle of the pond and that we needed help, before the line went dead again. I had heard Peter exclaim, 'Oh no!' so fingers crossed, I thought, he would come to our rescue.

The kids were tired, bored and hungry. In the distance we could see the lights of a fairground. May and Sidney offered to take the children off to the fair for a while. 'Good idea!' I said and settled down to watch the boat in the now murky water. The sky was becoming quite dark, it felt cold and the heath was deserted.

It seemed that May and co had only just left when I caught sight of them walking back to me again. Jemima had suddenly wanted to go to the loo again so they fled past me and straight back into the local pub to make a convenience of the toilets.

When we were all back together again I decided to give in, abandon the ship and go home, warm up and partake of a nice cup of tea. Blow this naval stuff. I felt like giving in and giving up on it all so I did just that. Sidney drove the children and me back to my house. I put the children to bed and rang Peter and Sally's house. Hearing Sally tell me that Peter had left for Blackheath pond. I was relieved to think that I might yet get my little boat back.

About an hour later a telephone call from a giggling May told me that the rescue operation had been successful. Thinking that I would still be with May and Sidney at their house, Peter had driven there to them with the rescued boat. Apparently, they found him standing at the door looking like a drowned rat. The pond had been much deeper than his waders allowed, with the water reaching to above his waist. Whilst he'd been in the middle of the pond bare chested, two mounted policemen stopped by and stared at him. Peter, realising that he had parked his car on a double yellow line, waited apprehensively to be ticked off or asked for his details. The officers continued to stare at him for a few moments and then rode away.

Apart from the obvious parking infringement, Peter wondered if it might be usual to see a seemingly naked man, wading in Blackheath pond in the darkness, up to his waist in water? Funny old world sometimes.

Chapter 20

Fin du livre

Dear Amanda,

Enclosing the first draft of 'The Book' and I guess that just wraps up everything that began in that strange interlude when I had to stop work. It is much better being back at work and 'Mrs Ordinary' again though I will never take good health for granted, nor the patience of my dear husband who, I have discovered, is quite 'Extra Ordinary' for putting up with me and for so many other reasons that I couldn't begin to list. I have no idea what the next few years or even the rest of life itself may bring but I have stopped caring about such things and now, and don't look too far ahead. I feel rather like a chrysalis on exit from a cocoon; asking myself just who was that strange person doing time inside it? If needing a reminder I could always go and have a few more needles stuck into my neck or stay a while at The Retreat Centre and perhaps sit on 'the staff table' for old times' sake. It might let off another fuse i.e. a spate of silly anecdotes and tales BUT the experience of becoming vulnerable, losing a job and in desperation finding my true self through those experiences has made a true and unforgettable mark on me.

St. Paul sums up best what I think in the book of Ecclesiastes:

> 'To everything there is a season
> And a time to every purpose under the heavens.'

Lovely isn't it, Amanda?

That was all a very long time ago... years in fact. Life changed, people passed away or out of my life. We came to the end of the millennium, experienced the Olympic Games in Britain, several World Cups and common use of emails and mobile phones, which I had little interest in using at the start of this collection of little snippets and tales.

Eventually, I gained my MA after a long and difficult period of disability, which should now be a distant memory. Instead, I think of the work focussed 'being' that I had allowed myself to become with a thought only for the present and immediate task in hand instead of the unique and transitory life that is the inheritance of us all. I still love to look, imagine and interpret the funny little interruptions of life and I have come to view my existence as an odd stew of other people's little snippets. Does this matter at all? No, not to me anyway. What has more impact is the love, laughs, pain and memory that hold significance, no matter from which direction they may come.

So, life moved on and time removed many of the souls important in life. My dear long suffering and strong-minded husband didn't make the age of sixty-four years, passing away shortly after dear eccentric (and much like me) uncle Sid. My mother acting true to form outlived both of them to reach her ninety-ninth year just short of a week and dear friend Julia followed a year later while her homeopathic enthusiast and miracle friend Emily, lived well past her hundredth year. Mrs Singh has sold her sweets and stationer's shop and Mr Gobi is partially retired from his pharmacy (though I notice there is still a queue of people waiting for him to dispense his pills or wisdom on the days he is available). Dear Dr B has left the surgery he was at for so many years and now concentrates on visiting the elderly in care homes. He once confided to me that he had a secret yen to join Medecin Sans Frontieres and I couldn't think of anyone more suited to dispense kind, calm advice and help with a smile, than he. On a home visit to my mother when she lived alone, Dr B once climbed through her lounge window complete with bicycle helmet to save her the trouble of opening the door. I am sure he did it more to amuse her, and Mum did in fact, look upon him as the son she never had. Shortly before M left this world, Dr B happened to be visiting the care home my mother resided in and I was able to call him to her room. He held her hand, smiled and spoke a few words to her. Although Mum was too weak and almost beyond life to speak, I knew she was aware of his presence and that he would have been a great comfort to her.

I am grateful to all those people for being in my life and to some, for simply occupying my empty mind and imagination at a very difficult period. They have helped to turn a negative experience into a positive one in terms of this book, even if only for therapeutic purposes.

Life changes, events become history, but love never dies. I am several years older, fatter and things don't quite work as well as they used to, but I still have most of my own teeth and for several years now have been into singing and generally enjoying life as a second time around grandmother. I believe too, that the quiet, patient Dr Ling is alive, semi-retired and enjoying walking expeditions. Which reminds me, time for one last letter:

Dear Dr Ling,

Just thought I would send you a copy of this collection of diatribe as it features some of your treatments. The snippets are, perhaps, better than nothing to show for several wasted years and months of my life that at times was only relieved by the hope of your treatments and the support of friends. Please don't be offended by anything you read as it is not all meant to be true (just most of it). Thank you for those therapeutic jabs which seemed to have released in me a bit more than the odd encephalin.

Enjoy your walks, Dr Ling, and take pleasure from the fact that you will never, ever have to put up with a patient like me again.

With very best wishes,
Jane Avril!